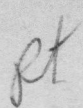

# "*If*, Lissa?"

She met his gaze unwaveringly. "I haven't said yes yet, Kane."

"Then why not say it?"

Lissa's heart fluttered a nervous protest, but she stuck to her guns. "There's too much unresolved between us. I'd rather work that through *before* we're married, *not* after."

Kane's face tightened. "No. You don't put me on trial. I will not be dangled. I'm either the man for you or I'm not."

"I'll think about it," she promised, recklessly pushing his patience to the limit.

She reached it.

"You don't have to think about it. You either do want to marry me or you don't."

"That's being totally unreasonable."

Kane didn't budge. "Make up your mind, Lissa. Now!"

**EMMA DARCY** nearly became an actress until her fiancé declared he preferred to attend the theater *with* her. She became a wife and mother. Later, she took up oil painting—unsuccessfully, she remarks. Then she tried architecture, designing the family home in New South Wales. Next came romance writing—"the hardest and most challenging of all the activities," she confesses.

## Books by Emma Darcy

### HARLEQUIN PRESENTS
1401—RIDE THE STORM
1433—BREAKING POINT
1447—HIGH RISK
1455—TO TAME A WILD HEART
1463—THE WEDDING
1472—THE SEDUCTION OF KEIRA

### HARLEQUIN ROMANCE
2900—BLIND DATE
2941—WHIRLPOOL OF PASSION
3085—PATTERN OF DECEIT

Don't miss any of our special offers. Write to us at the following address for information on our newest releases.

Harlequin Reader Service
P.O. Box 1397, Buffalo, NY 14240
Canadian address: P.O. Box 603,
Fort Erie, Ont. L2A 5X3

# EMMA DARCY

## The Velvet Tiger

**Harlequin Books**

TORONTO • NEW YORK • LONDON
AMSTERDAM • PARIS • SYDNEY • HAMBURG
STOCKHOLM • ATHENS • TOKYO • MILAN
MADRID • WARSAW • BUDAPEST • AUCKLAND

If you purchased this book without a cover you should be aware that this book is stolen property. It was reported as "unsold and destroyed" to the publisher, and neither the author nor the publisher has received any payment for this "stripped book."

Harlequin Presents first edition October 1992
ISBN 0-373-11496-6

THE VELVET TIGER

Copyright © 1992 by Emma Darcy. All rights reserved.
Except for use in any review, the reproduction or utilization
of this work in whole or in part in any form by any electronic,
mechanical or other means, now known or hereafter invented,
including xerography, photocopying and recording,
or in any information storage or retrieval system, is forbidden without
the permission of the publisher, Harlequin Enterprises Limited,
225 Duncan Mill Road, Don Mills, Ontario, Canada M3B 3K9.

All the characters in this book have no existence outside the
imagination of the author and have no relation whatsoever to
anyone bearing the same name or names. They are not even
distantly inspired by any individual known or unknown to the
author, and all incidents are pure invention.

® are Trademarks registered in the United States Patent and
Trademark Office and in other countries.

Printed in U.S.A.

# CHAPTER ONE

THE CALL CAME at ten-thirteen on Friday morning.
Lissa noted the time on the office clock and watched
several seconds click by as she absorbed the pleasurable shock of hearing Kane's voice. It took a few more
seconds before she remembered she had decided to
finish with him. For good. Completely, utterly, irre-
vocably.

Lissa cranked her determination up a few more
notches. It was not that Kane Marriott was all bad.
Quite the opposite, in many respects. He was wildly
handsome, wildly exciting and wildly dangerous—in
so far as he had blown away all the principles Lissa
had lived by before she met him. Being with Kane
made a lot of sane common sense seem totally irrelevant. But that wasn't the problem. The problem was
the way he treated her.

Worst of all was his indifference to what she was
thinking, or the way she thought, the almost contemptuous disregard for her frame of mind, her attitudes, everything that meant something to her. He did
what *he* wanted when *he* wanted. Her wants were
never consulted or considered. If they didn't coincide

with his, tough luck! And to Lissa that simply wasn't good enough.

She had given Kane Marriott a year of her life. More than long enough to determine they were going nowhere. Worse than nowhere. Staying with him robbed her of the chance of forging a happier relationship with some other man. A relationship that acknowledged there were *two* sides to it!

Three weeks of silence had been the last straw. Three long, dragging weeks during which Kane had not thought of her, or had decided he didn't want to spend a few minutes on a personal call. Which spelled out precisely where Lissa Gilmore came in his life. She was simply a convenience who hadn't been convenient while he was a thousand kilometres away. Since she wasn't giving him what he wanted, she was not worth spending his time on.

Each day that passed without one word from Kane had steeled Lissa's resolution to break off with him. Even now, when it did suit him to remember her existence, he was calling during business hours, which prevented any possibility of talking on a personal level.

Not that Kane ever indulged in long chats of a personal nature. And if he were to indulge in that activity, Lissa knew him well enough to know it would not be by telephone. Kane preferred to use his hands. And his eyes. And his mouth. His disembodied voice did not have the full seductive impact of his physical presence. The telephone had little appeal to Kane

Marriott. Communication by that instrument was always short and to the point. No frills.

Despite all this, simply hearing his voice made a mishmash of Lissa's resolutions. Not all the reasonable logic in the world took away the fact that Kane made her feel special in a way no other man ever did. While her mind seethed through all the reasons she should tell him to get lost, jump into the nearest lake or simply go to hell, every nerve in her body leapt with anticipation at the thought of seeing him again. Being with him again.

"I expect to have everything settled here by this afternoon, Lissa," he was saying. He sounded tired. "Which means," he continued, "we'll be able to have the whole weekend together. I'm not sure yet what flight I'll catch from Melbourne, so it would probably be best if we meet at my apartment."

Of course, Lissa thought sourly. That would save time. For him. For what he wanted from her. His apartment meant his bed. Any other kind of communication was not on Kane Marriott's agenda. not where a woman was concerned. Especially not where Lissa Gilmore was concerned.

Kane had only one real priority in his life—the success of his engineering company. His was straight-line motivation. Nothing interfered, nothing deterred him. Lissa could see all too clearly where she fit in.

A crisis at his construction site in Victoria had taken him away, and undoubtedly some other business necessity was bringing him back. That gave him a free weekend to slot Lissa into her accustomed position.

The only purpose or importance a woman had to him was to provide relief and recreation from work pressure. Now that Kane was returning to Sydney, he was lining Lissa up for tonight's R and R.

That thought did not thrill her. Indeed, it had exactly the opposite effect. It doused the treacherous fever that coursed through her blood at the mere sound of his voice. Kane Marriott didn't deserve such a response from her, and Lissa fiercely resented the chemistry he stirred. It wasn't fair he could still do that when he'd proved he didn't care for her.

"Did it ever occur to you that you should ask me nicely?"

Silence at the other end of the line. Lissa imagined Kane gnashing his teeth in annoyed impatience. Let him, she thought mutinously.

"I am asking you nicely," he said belatedly and brusquely.

"No, you're not."

A vexed sigh. "Well, let's start again." His voice sounded even more weary, although it now had an edge of irritation. "I am asking you nicely to meet me after the flight at my apartment."

"No. I won't be meeting you there, Kane," Lissa said succinctly. She was not going to be the stand-by bed mate tonight. Or any other night.

"Why not?" he demanded sharply.

That snapped him out of his weary condescension, Lissa thought with grim satisfaction. "I'm busy," she replied. Every bit as busy as he had been for the last three weeks, and on innumerable other occasions.

The silence at the other end of the line was longer this time. She wondered if it was the silence of shock— eager, compliant Lissa was not a lay-down certainty after all. She savagely hoped it had jolted him out of his insulting complacency.

His response, when it came, was a hard rasp of suspicion. "With another man?"

Lissa fumed. Of course, Kane wouldn't relate any fault to himself. She wondered if his suspicion had its basis in his own sins. When he was away on business, did he find someone else to accommodate him? Was that why he never called, except to say when he would be home? Lissa wasn't at all sure she hadn't been sharing Kane with other women all along.

"Perhaps," she said, her wounded pride recklessly feeding what could only be a destructive suspicion. I've done it now, she thought. This is the beginning of the end.

She heard him swear under his breath. It wasn't a nice word. Then in a burst of frustration, "What the hell are you playing at, Lissa? Don't give me the hard-to-get routine. I warn you, I've no patience with it."

"No, I'm sure you haven't, Kane," she said bitterly. "But there comes a time when all the accommodating doesn't fall your way from me."

"There's not enough time for this damned nonsense," he grated. "Whatever devious little game you've got on your mind, forget it! If you don't want to be with me, just say so, Lissa."

And that would be that, she thought, a sinking pit in her stomach. The cut-off point was staring her in the face. From *him!* No argument. No apology. No "give me another chance and I'll be different, Lissa." Those words would never fall from Kane's lips. He only ever held out a plain simple equation—you either want me or you don't.

She did.

That was plain and simple.

Except she wanted a lot more from Kane Marriott than he was prepared to give.

Some game, she thought bitterly. He made the rules. He was the referee. He blew the whistle. And there was no talking back about any decisions he made. How she could love a man like that was beyond all reason! He didn't give a damn about her feelings.

"It's no game to me, Kane. I'm calling it off. We're finished. No more time for anything."

There! She'd said the words. She hadn't expected to say them here and now. They had slipped out under emotional duress. A totally unplanned finale that felt dreadfully wrong. Although she had made the decision to end their relationship, she had meant to see Kane again, to tell him face to face. At least go out with a bang, not a whimper!

"Lissa?" No harshness in his voice now. More a strained uncertainty. "You don't mean that?"

What point was there in postponing the inevitable? So it made her feel ill. It still had to be done. "Yes, I do," she said dully.

A hesitation, then more sharply, "You can't mean it!"

"I'm sorry, but I do," she said more firmly. She was sorry. Genuinely sorry. A huge void was opening up in her life. What have I done? she wondered. What have I done? "I'm sorry," she repeated as a host of buzzing uncertainties attacked her resolution.

"You're sorry!" he drawled in bitter derision. "That's marvellous. Bloody marvellous! I've been burning my brains out, day in, day out, and you... Oh, go to hell!" he cursed her, and slammed the receiver down.

The thud of the telephone on the hook was like the last ominous beat of a dying heart. Her head told her she had done the right thing. Her emotions were completely screwed up, twisting and churning through her stomach. She fumbled down her own receiver and looked at her hands. The long delicate fingers were trembling in harmony with her troubled thoughts.

Kane had acted true to form. Cursing her in anger and frustration at having his convenience removed so abruptly and unexpectedly. Yet the sense of loss burrowing through her was equally unbearable.

She loved him. And she wanted him. But both the love and the wanting hurt because of what he had been doing to her. She was not a rag doll for Kane Marriott to play with, to pick up and toss aside as he saw fit. She was a person, and the way he treated her had been eating away at her self-esteem for months. She'd had to end it.

But not like this, she mourned. Not with this bleak ache of nothingness, as though all her limbs had been severed. She couldn't even cry. She was beyond tears.

Maybe it was shock, she thought. She felt numb all over. Lifeless. As though there was nothing to look forward to ever again.

She looked around her spacious and tastefully furnished office. She held a prestigious position—secretary to the managing director of the Australian branch of ICAC, a huge international conglomerate—and her working conditions could hardly be bettered. Excellent pay. She met a lot of important and powerful people. Yet none of it seemed to matter.

The void grew bigger and darker.

*This is despair,* she thought. *But I'll get over it eventually. I'm only twenty-four years old. All I have to do is wipe out this last year with Kane Marriott and start afresh. One day some man will come along— someone entirely different to Kane—someone who will value me as a person and not just as a responsive female body.*

"Everything ready for this afternoon's board meeting, Lissa?"

The question jolted her out of her dark introspection. She looked up at her boss, who virtually filled the doorway between their offices with his big frame. Jack Conway was a big man in every way, a bull of a man who had no hesitation about squashing inefficient underlings. He hadn't arrived at the managing directorship by being tolerant of people who didn't carry their load of responsibilities.

"Yes, sir," she replied crisply. She had laid everything out ready in the boardroom first thing this morning, making certain that she wasn't caught out by any unpredictable hitches.

He gave a short nod of satisfaction. His steel-grey eyes glinted with a different kind of satisfaction as they appraised her appearance. As usual, her blue-black hair rippled neatly away from her temples, framing her oval face and long neck with a dark shining abundance of waves and curls that swirled to her shoulders. She wore a violet dress that hugged the soft curves of her figure and highlighted the purple of her thickly fringed eyes. The hint of mauve in her lipstick was subtly repeated in the blusher she used to touch up her cheekbones. Her delicately arched eyebrows were as exquisitely feminine as her finely shaped nose and her small, even teeth.

She flashed a wry little smile at her boss. When she had first started working for him, Lissa had felt quite discomfited by his habit of looking her over each day. She had left her previous job because things had started getting sticky with her employer, who thought no meant he had to try harder. Jack Conway, however, had perceived her suspicions and summarily dismissed them.

"My dear girl, I am fifty-four years old and past the age of playing around," he had drawled sardonically, the steel-grey eyes glinting with amusement. "At this time in my life, I prefer to direct my energies elsewhere. To me you are an asset. I enjoy having assets."

She had believed his blunt declaration of disinterest, and the past two years of working with him had borne out the truth of it. Jack Conway did see her appearance as an asset, and Lissa suspected that was the reason he had selected her ahead of other applicants for the job of his secretary.

He was oddly possessive of her, but not in any sexual or paternal sense. It was more a power play. She was an extension of him, and her "class," as he called it, was both a status symbol as well as a useful distraction to other men in business meetings. Jack Conway was not above using anything or anyone to seize an advantage.

"That colour is very striking on you," he commented approvingly. "You should wear it more often, Lissa."

"Thank you, sir," she said, aware that he was filing it away for future reference.

A knowing little smile curved his lips as he turned to his office.

Jack Conway used every edge available to him in his business negotiations. He was never distracted by her presence at meetings, but other men were. Occasionally, he would ask her to wear a particular dress on a certain day. It invariably coincided with a tricky negotiation. When Lissa had eventually cottoned on to Jack Conway's purpose, she didn't know whether to be offended or amused. She finally decided it didn't really matter.

With a sense of bitter irony she reflected that Kane Marriott was one of the few men who had not fallen for the trick. She vividly remembered her first meeting with him, the feeling of eyes watching her, de-

vouring her with sharp intensity. She had looked up
from the work on her desk and he had been poised in
the doorway, totally still, yet emanating an almost
magnetic energy. Then very slowly his mouth had
curved into a smile that made every nerve in her body
tingle with electric life.

It was she who had been totally distracted by him
throughout his subsequent meeting with Jack Conway. Kane's mind had not wavered one iota from the
business under discussion. Although she had sat in on
the meeting and taken notes, not once had he looked
her way or shown any awareness of her presence. His
concentration on what he wanted to achieve had been
absolute until he had won the agreement on the contract he was angling for. Then, and only then, did he
turn his attention to Lissa, and his eyes had known she
was his for the asking.

As plain and as simple as that.

She had been such an easy conquest for him. And
the crazy part was, she had never plunged straight into
a love affair before and would never have believed it
of herself if anyone had predicted it a year ago. But it
had all been so different with Kane. Caution hadn't
entered her head. Somehow he had generated a compelling excitement that broke all barriers, that didn't
recognise barriers existed.

No wonder he had taken her compliance for
granted. She had never refused him anything he
wanted of her. He had only to look at her with those
vibrant, compelling eyes and she had no defences at all
against the power of his desires.

Her only chance of breaking that power was to remove herself from his radius. So perhaps it had been best to end it on the telephone instead of dragging out the agony. Yet not to see him again... Sheer anguish stabbed through her heart. Why couldn't he have loved her as she loved him? Why...?

The telephone on her desk rang again. She picked it up from force of habit, then had to work hard at producing a calm, pleasant tone of voice. "ICAC head office. Lissa Gilmore speaking. How can I help you?" she rattled out with creditable aplomb.

"This is Kane."

"Oh!"

Her throat instantly tightened up, strangling any possibility of producing further words. Incredulity billowed through her mind. Kane making an effort to come back to her? Wanting her enough to pursue her past a flat rejection? Her whole body clenched with treacherous anticipation.

"Please don't hang up." It was a command, but at least he was giving her the courtesy of a "please."

Lissa's mind wavered between hope and bitter scepticism. She swallowed hard, opened up a passage for sound and voiced a terse reminder. "You just did that to me, Kane."

"I'm sorry. I was...impetuous."

Which was a fine euphemism for foul-tempered. However, apologies from Kane were so rare that Lissa held her fire.

"Is this an *impetuous* call, Kane? Because if it is—"

"No! I want to speak to you."

"What about?"

"You're being impetuous, too."

"No, I'm not."

"You don't think it's impetuous to blow away a year-long intimacy on the phone, Lissa?"

Her self-respect demanded that she not pull any punches, even though he was holding out a chance for her to change her mind and have him back. She wanted him. Desperately. But not the way it was.

"Let's call that an intermittent intimacy, where you do all the calling of the intermissions. In your own selfish time and in an insufferably demanding way. I don't like being treated like that, Kane. And I'm not going to let you treat me like that."

"In short, I wasn't being *nice* enough for you," he mocked.

Lissa's hackles instantly rose. "If you want to see it that way—"

"No, hold it!" he whipped in quickly. "Let's take this weekend to talk about it, Lissa."

She knew precisely what kind of talking he wanted to do. He was simply angling to get her into his bed. "You don't want to listen, Kane," she accused bitterly.

"Give it a chance, Lissa," he came back smoothly, persuasively. "At least try for a reconciliation."

"Why?"

"Because we're good together."

She couldn't deny that. Temptation quivered seductively through her body at the thought of making love with him again. Would there ever be anyone else as good as Kane?

"I think we've had enough goodness together," she forced out harshly, angry with herself for being so weak. She wanted, needed more from Kane than his raw sensuality.

"One more time? Just a few days, Lissa. Just to be certain?" he pressed softly, insidiously.

She wavered. What did a few more days matter?

"Meet me at the apartment and I'll give you a surprise," he added swiftly, as though he sensed a weakening.

"What surprise?" she demanded suspiciously.

He gave a soft little laugh. "It wouldn't be a surprise if I told you, Lissa."

It was the laugh that pulled her up. Kane thought he had her in his hands again. Putty to be moulded to his will. "No. I won't come to your apartment, Kane."

"Why not?"

"Because you'll want to tumble me straight into bed."

"That's not a bad idea," he purred, using his voice to full effect now, a sensual caress that evoked all the pleasurable things he could do to her. And would do. With his hands, and his mouth, and . . .

Lissa gritted her teeth. "It's not on," she bit out, determined not to be drawn into *his* game, where there were no rules except his.

A wistful sigh. A projection of softness that Lissa knew was totally false. There was no softness in Kane

Marriott. "What can I do to change your mind?" he asked in a tone of whimsical appeal.

She had to admire the way he could concentrate his mind on doing whatever he had to do to win. It was a formidable skill. "Nothing," Lissa said stubbornly, resenting the glib way he could change tack to suit his purpose. Yet for once he was making an effort on *her* behalf.

"Except?" he slid back, undeterred by her brick-wall defence.

"Except what?"

"There's always an except. Be merciful, my sweet, soft, darling Lissa, and tell me what the except is, because I cannot envisage the rest of my life without you."

He meant this weekend without her. Lissa wasn't fooled. Kane Marriott didn't need her—not her, the person. He didn't need anyone. Kane was a completely self-contained man. A self-made man. And answerable to no-one. It was probably that quality in him that made him so attractive, so exciting, so challenging to women. Along with the air of assurance that telegraphed the attitude, "I'll dare anything, and more times than not I'll get away with it."

Nothing to lose and everything to gain... that was Kane Marriott. She knew him so well. Too well. He was not about to change to accommodate her needs, and for a lifetime relationship Lissa needed more than Kane's kind of loving. But for just another few days...

Weak, she thought. Weak and stupid to give in to him when she knew perfectly well it would lead to nothing new. Nothing different or better between them. To have this weekend with Kane was an indulgence of the worst kind. He didn't love her. Never had. She would simply be letting him use her once again because . . . because she wanted one more memory of what it was like with him—good and bad.

Then she would get on with her life.

Without him.

"I'll meet you at the airport," she said.

"Lissa, I don't know what flight I'll be on."

"Ring me and tell me the schedule," she insisted, digging her heels in on this point. He was not going to have everything his own way. Not this last weekend.

"Why not meet at the apartment?"

"Because I want to talk to you first. And if the talking isn't good, Kane, I might not get to your apartment."

"All right," he conceded grudgingly. "I'll be on the 6:05."

"I thought you didn't know which flight you'd be on."

"I just made up my mind."

"How nice! Thank you for reminding me what an absolute bastard you are when it comes to getting your own way," Lissa remarked acidly.

"Being nice doesn't pay, Lissa," he returned dryly.

"The lesson has been learnt, Kane. One day you might rue it," she retorted, then hung up on him.

# CHAPTER TWO

LISSA MADE A CONSCIOUS effort to relax the tension that was mangling her nerves and cramping her stomach. She was running late. It wasn't her fault that the board meeting had been an extra-long session that had not broken up until after five o'clock. Then there had been all the filing to do before she could leave the office. And now the traffic, moving at a snail's pace!

Kane's business had always come first with him, Lissa argued to herself. How many times had he kept her waiting while he finished what he had to finish? He had kept her waiting for three whole weeks! Let him have a taste of his own medicine, she thought savagely.

If he so much as criticised her for being late meeting his flight she would—she would . . . A harsh laugh broke from her throat as she realised she would do nothing. The reason her nerves were on edge and her stomach clenching was that she believed Kane Marriott would not wait for her. As soon as he realised she wasn't there to meet him . . . No, Kane Marriott wouldn't wait for her.

It was all so one-sided. Whatever Kane did was always right. If she stepped one millimetre off line, no matter for what reason, she was wrong. Lissa fumed at herself. It was so weak of her to carry on. She should stand Kane up. Turn the car around and simply go home.

Her eyes flicked once more to the clock on the dashboard. Six twenty-two. Her fingers worked agitatedly around the steering wheel as she waited for the red light ahead to change to green. Maybe she would get through this hellish intersection on the next surge forward. Her foot hovered impatiently on the accelerator. The traffic snarl at the Oxford Street intersection was always horrendous at peak hour, but Friday evenings were absolute chaos. It would be another twenty minutes at least before she could get to the airport terminal.

It was sheer stupidity on her part to keep on going. But she had said she would meet him at the airport, so she would turn up, even if he wasn't there.

And if he wasn't there, that was that, Lissa decided. She was not going to pursue him to his apartment. No way! She wouldn't give Kane that satisfaction ever again. If he wanted this last weekend with her—to try for a reconciliation—he had better be at the airport waiting. No matter how late she was! After all, she had good reason to be late.

This was a test of his sincerity.

Lissa's mouth curled into a cynical smile.

Or perhaps it was more like a test of how much he wanted the relief and recreation that she provided. After three weeks he should be well and truly frustrated. If he wasn't cheating her on the side.

The realisation came that he could easily find someone else. That would never be a problem to Kane Marriott. He could have women falling over him at the drop of a hat. One inviting flash of those wickedly knowing eyes would be sufficient to draw practically anyone to his side.

But they were *good* together. And Kane, being the sensualist he was, would not be content with anything less than the response he drew from her. If he wanted that badly enough—tonight—then he would wait.

Of course, they had had a year to discover all the varied ways of pleasing each other. Intensely. Kane would undoubtedly consider it a large investment of his time and expertise and might want his return for it. She began to wonder how far he would go to keep what he had with her.

Lissa had considered what they shared together as loving. It had taken a long time for disillusionment to set in. Which was why she had never thought of withholding sex from Kane, or using it as a lever to force him to come her way. Yet maybe that was the only kind of language Kane understood. And if that was the case, she was far better off without him.

Where had all her giving got her with Kane? No farther than his bed! That's where! She was definitely far better off without him!

What had he said?

*Sweet, soft, darling Lissa?*

*Well, not any more, my dear, hard, ruthless Kane,* she silently promised him.

The traffic light turned green.

The trip out to Mascot took even longer than Lissa had estimated. It was six-fifty by the time she found a parking space, and it was another five minutes before she walked into the domestic terminal where Kane would be waiting for her. If he was still there.

Her eyes darted frantically around the milling crowd. The terminal was packed with people either preparing to fly out or having just flown in for the weekend. If Kane was watching the entrances, he was far more likely to see her first, she thought, so she stood still, hoping he would spot her. But she saw him before he saw her.

As always, her heart jolted at first sight of him, then began beating at an accelerated pace. It didn't seem to matter how stupid and self-destructive it was to love him. She did. A soft warmth flowed through her whole body just looking at him. It was incredibly difficult to find any steel to put into her backbone.

Kane Marriott stood out from the crowd. He had the personal charisma that stamped him as an individual, sufficient unto himself, and the rest of mankind only existed for him to rise above them. They didn't touch him.

Passers-by glanced at him, drawn by that indefinable air of separation from the hustle and bustle around him. Women took a second look. Women would always take a second look at Kane Marriott. Apart from being wildly handsome, he exuded a virility that was all male animal, the ultimate threat and promise of what the mating game was all about. His tall and muscular physique suggested brute domination, but his eyes and mouth denied any brutality except that which was eagerly welcomed and deliciously exciting.

*The velvet tiger.* The words had stuck in her mind from a movie she had seen. A good description of Kane. Or rather a good description of the sexuality he emitted. Not his colouring. A panther better described his colouring.

His hair was black and thick and sleekly shiny. It dipped over his broad forehead in an attractive way, drawing attention to the emphatic black slashes of eyebrows that had a wickedly challenging kick at their ends. His eyes were deep-set and totally riveting. They were almost black, and they could mesmerise with sparkling brilliance or melt into hot chocolate with dark swirling passion. His nose was strong, not quite hawkish but decisively masculine. As was his squarish jaw line. Sharply defined, prominent bones. Which made his mouth all the more fascinating because it was so sensually moulded, provocative in the fullness of his lower lip and exciting in the elongated curve of the upper one.

His fine white linen shirt was carelessly unbuttoned to halfway down his chest, revealing the dark arrow of hair that curled from his smoothly tanned skin. He had his hands jammed into the pockets of a black leather jacket, its fashionable style severely thrown out of balance by the action. Not that Kane would care about that. He bought the best on principle, but he wore it how he pleased. His superbly tailored black trousers fitted him to perfection. As undoubtedly did his Italian leather shoes. Gucci luggage sat near his feet. Kane Marriott liked to show he had made it to the top.

That thought made Lissa wonder if Kane viewed her as a status symbol, just as Jack Conway did. She instantly discarded the idea. Kane wasn't interested in showing her off. He had never cared about what clothes she wore when they socialised. He always had been far more interested in getting them off her at the end of the evening. No, there was only one thing Kane wanted her for. Being *good* together.

She saw his head turning, slowly scanning the crowd. His eyes found her and instantly sharpened to black probing darts that would have pinned her to a wall if there had been one behind her. Gone was the indifferent look. She could almost see an electric charge go through his body, priming his vitality to a high-pressure level.

Rebellion sent a charge through her body. If he blasted her for keeping him waiting, she would turn on her heel and march right out on him. Whether this was somehow telegraphed to him, Lissa didn't know. His face tightened to grim purpose for a moment, then visibly relaxed. He did not smile.

She found herself so tense that she couldn't smile at him, either. She simply stared at him, her heart squeezing tighter and tighter. The crowd around them, between them, blurred into non-existence. In some indefinable sense she felt that she belonged to this man, always had, always would. She might tear herself away from him, but she would never forget him.

Some part of her would always be his. He had commanded it from the very beginning, and nothing—not distance, not time, not the most determined resolution—was ever going to change that. He was wrong for her. Yet somehow he was right for her, too.

Kane picked up his bags and walked towards her, long, lithe strides that closed the distance between them with economical swiftness. His eyes held hers all the way, commanding her to stay right where she was. Tension swirled from him, locking her to him, his vitality, his purpose for her, no matter what that purpose was.

Lissa didn't move. She had neither the strength nor the will to counter the deep well of need that Kane Marriott both stirred and left tantalisingly unanswered. He was good, all right. Good at turning her into a quivering mess of desires craving for fulfilment. From him.

He dropped his bags and reached for her in the same motion, enclosing her in his arms, pressing her body to his as if nothing had happened between them, as if she weren't incredibly late.... As if he loved her and wanted no-one else but her and all was forgiven.... As if all of him was hungry for the feel of her, the softness of her, the easy giving that he took for granted and now took again as though it was his by right.

Lissa could feel his heart beating faster than usual. The hand he thrust through her hair to tilt her head to his was not gentle. And the eyes that bored down into hers were turbulent with questions instead of twinkling with love and loving. He hadn't liked waiting. He hadn't liked it one bit.

He kissed her hard, wanting to smash the barriers she had raised, wanting to dominate again. A stab of angry pride made Lissa keep her lips closed. Kane was not going to have it easy with her this time. All take and no give. She wanted to feel loved, not ravaged into submission.

She forced herself to resist his storming kiss until he softened the pressure against her mouth, teased her lips apart, stirred soft thrilling tingles and wooed her into the response that was exploding inside her, uncontainable. Her hands crept up over his shoulders, around his neck, and clung as though she were drowning. Which she was. In the sensations he aroused with slow but passionate intent. He won what he wanted from her. Total submission. Then his eyes blazed through the swimming dark purple of her emotional turmoil.

"You're late," he rasped, as though something inside him had been scraped raw at the thought that she might not be coming at all.

"I didn't think you'd wait," she blurted out, desperately wanting to believe that she *was* important to him and he needed her in his life.

"I did wait," he pointed out with some asperity.

*Because he cares about me? As deeply as I care about him?* The questions tortured Lissa's mind as she gave her excuse. "I was held up at a board meeting."

His eyebrows met in a frown. "What were they deciding?" he asked, smoothing his voice into a languid tone that suggested boredom.

Lissa knew that tone. Kane used it as camouflage when something was vitally important to him. Like the decisions made at an ICAC board meeting. Which, of course, would be much more important than she was. A bitter jealousy poisoned the hopes she had allowed into her heart and mind.

"Various things," she answered evasively.

The frown slowly ironed itself out. She could almost see the decision form in his mind. He would find out about that later. Deal with Lissa first. What had happened at the board meeting was not going to go away. She might.

His mouth curled into a sensual taunt. The dark eyes glinted their wicked knowingness. "Your choice of meeting place is hardly appropriate, Lissa. Too public. I hope you're more satisfied with it than I am."

His hand splayed over the small of her back, holding her to him, deliberately reminding her of the explosive impact that meeting each other always had.

"Too public for what?" she whispered, knowing he meant sex—knowing it, but desperately wanting him to deny that was all he wanted with her.

"What we do best together."

*He* did not realise it, but his words were almost a death knell. "You've controlled your need for three weeks, Kane. You can manage a little bit longer," she replied, the sarcasm furred by a thousand other feelings.

Desire simmered hotly in his eyes. "Who wants to?"

"I do," Lissa answered coldly. She unlinked her hands from around his neck and dragged them down to his chest.

Desire glittered into derision. He untangled the hand in her hair, slid it down the curve of her spine, then gripped her waist with both hands, spanning it with a possessive and dominant strength. She had shown him how vulnerable she still was to his physical attraction, and he had no compunction about pressing that advantage.

"Let's get on our way," he said brusquely. "I need a drink. I need food. I need you. And I want to know what went on in that board meeting that was so important you kept me waiting an hour."

Lissa ignored the reference to drink, food and sex. That listing was all too predictable. She ignored the reference to the information he wanted for his precious business, as well. That, too, was eminently predictable. Her seething resentments fastened on the waiting as a bone of contention. It represented the straw that would break them.

Her eyes flashed bitter rebellion. "You resent being held up by me, don't you?"

"Yes, I do." No tempering of his resentment. No compromising from Kane Marriott.

"But you don't mind keeping me waiting."

"You know that's different," he dismissed with all the ingrained arrogance she had come to hate.

"No, it's not," she bit out angrily.

His face tightened. A muscle twitched along his jaw line. The dark eyes flared a warning. "Is this your idea of getting back at me, Lissa?" he asked softly.

"Why would I want to do that?" she challenged him. "Since you never do any wrong."

The warning hardened. "You're making reconciliation as difficult as possible."

"How? All I'm asking is for you to be reasonable."

"I am. I'm always reasonable. That's why I've got to where I am."

"I was unavoidably detained."

"You could have rung the airport. Left a message. Met me at my apartment. You deliberately kept me waiting here, Lissa," he accused.

She hadn't thought of ringing the airport. In her heart of hearts she hadn't believed he would wait. But she didn't want to confess those failings. "You kept me waiting for three weeks. You didn't give a damn about letting me know how long you'd be."

His jaw clenched. "I didn't know how long I'd be. And I've no time for people who make things difficult for the sake of being difficult. If this is your idea of trying to reach an understanding..."

"If that's how you want to judge me," she snapped, "I can't see how we'll ever reach an understanding."

His eyes blazed with violent impatience. "Lissa, make your mind up now. Do you want me in your life or not? If you don't—" he nodded to where she had come in ''—there's the exit out of the terminal, and out of my life.''

He picked his hands off her waist. She was free to go. She dropped her hands from his chest. Pride screamed at her to go now, to defy all that he was and walk away. But the power and the passion of the man swirled around her, sucking her into a vortex of needs and desires that denied her any freedom, and a black empty void hovered in her mind's eye. Despair pleaded that she shouldn't be hasty. Kane was irritable from having been kept waiting, but he *had* waited. Even though she hadn't called, as she could have done, if she'd thought of it. And she herself was overwrought from too much inner turmoil. She took a deep breath to calm herself.

''I'm prepared to try it,'' she said, ''for this last weekend. Then I'll see. I'll make my decision Sunday night.''

''So will I,'' he snapped at her.

''What does that mean?''

He didn't answer. He took a long, deep breath. The air he breathed out seemed to shimmer with the heat of banked passions he was determined to control. Something like pain twisted across his face before he smoothed it into a stony expression that revealed nothing of his inner thoughts and feelings. He stooped and picked up a tissue-wrapped bundle that had fallen beside his suitcase. He thrust it into her hands. A brusque, angry gesture rather than a giving one.

Puzzled, she parted the layers of tissue. It was a posy of massed violets. She laughed out of sheer nervous reaction to the gift and the way he had presented it. "God, you're hopeless, Kane!" she said, shaking her head in bemused reproach. "Is this supposed to be my surprise?"

His eyes stabbed black resentment at her. "One of them," he said grimly. "I've never done it before."

"No. You never have," she said quietly, looking at him with wondering eyes, searching for the meaning she might have missed because of her own churning emotions.

He had never given her anything personal, never anything especially for her. He had taken her out to dinners, shows, nightclubs, totally unconcerned about the extravagant amount of money he spent on pleasures and entertainments they shared together. But romantic gestures such as flowers or other little gifts had never formed any part of their relationship. She doubted it had ever formed part of any relationship he had had. Frills were definitely not Kane's style.

*Never before!*

So why now?

Flowers to sweeten her up after the sourness of this morning's phone call? Flowers to get his own way with her? But wouldn't he think roses would suit that purpose better? Violets were a far more personal choice, as though he truly had been thinking of her, Lissa, a special person to him, not just a convenience, someone for whom he had made an exception against his rule.

"Thank you, Kane," she said softly, hopefully.

The tightness around his mouth relaxed into a self-mocking little smile. "Any man can be a fool once in a while."

"It's not unmanly to give a woman flowers," she gently chided, realising why the posy had been smothered in tissue paper. This concession went totally against his grain, a symbol of weakness to him, a measure of feeling for her that perhaps went deeper than desire.

"Don't count on its becoming a habit," he growled, and bent to pick up his bags.

Lissa told herself she was crazy to make so much of it, but as she led Kane towards her car, she couldn't help taking more and more pleasure from the posy of violets, caressing the tightly clustered flowers with a light finger touch, lifting it to her nose to breathe in its scent over and over again. If Kane had wanted to give her an aphrodisiac, he could not have chosen better.

Did he know?

Was it deliberately planned?

He had never done it before.

But then she had never been difficult before.

Being nice didn't pay, she reminded herself.

She darted a searching glance at Kane as he strode along beside her. He had a dark brooding look on his face. Not planned, she decided. If anything, he had acted against his better judgment and was vexed with himself as well as with her.

Lissa smiled. She had actually won a victory. A small one, but a victory nevertheless. What it meant was highly questionable, but she had the weekend to find out. She decided to find out a lot of things this weekend. Maybe it was possible to right what was wrong. At least some of it. Enough to make their relationship better. Perhaps worth going on with.

Two days should be more than sufficient to see if there truly was a chance of reconciliation. Lissa looked ahead, saw the coming conflicts that had to be faced and resolved. It was going to be one hell of a weekend.

## CHAPTER THREE

THEY REACHED THE CAR. Lissa took her key ring from her handbag, unlocked the boot and opened it for Kane to stow his bags. He tossed them in, closed the boot and commandeered the keys.

"I'll drive," he said, moving to the passenger side to unlock the door for her.

"It's my car," Lissa reminded him tersely, niggled by his presumption.

He paused and sent her a mocking look. "It will be quicker if I drive."

"I don't want to go fast."

She stepped around the car and pointedly held out her hand for the keys, determined that Kane was not going to run this weekend by his rules.

He heaved a weary sigh. "What do you want from me, Lissa?"

Everything that a man in love would give the woman he loves, Lissa thought. Some caring consideration would make up for a lot of other sins. So would some respect for her wishes. But Kane was not in the mood to tolerate a barrage of criticism from her. His air of studied patience had that quality of stillness prevalent in the eye of a hurricane.

One thing at a time, she cautioned herself. Since Kane prided himself on being reasonable, she had to attack with reason. "For a start," she said, keeping her tone low and calm, "I want to know why you didn't bother ringing me all the time you were away."

"I told you I had a crisis on my hands," came the flat reply.

"Every minute of every day? Including weekends?" she asked, unable to keep an edge of scepticism out of her voice.

"Yes."

"You couldn't spare even five minutes?"

"What for, Lissa?"

"To talk to me. To let me know you hadn't completely forgotten me."

"I rang you today. I'm here because I didn't forget you."

"That's not the point."

"What is the point?"

Her eyes wavered from his. She could feel a rush of hot blood scorching her cheeks. She had never asked him before, and she hated asking now, but she wanted—needed—to know. If he had been unfaithful to her, she could not turn a blind eye to that, no matter how much she loved him and wanted to be with him. She forced her gaze to his, defiantly challenging.

"Have you been with anyone else on these business trips, Kane?"

He shook his head as though he couldn't believe she had harboured such a suspicion. His dark eyes derided the vulnerable anxiety in hers. "Is that what this is all about, Lissa?"

Not all, she thought, but she didn't answer him. She waited, watching for any flicker of evasion, her body aching with tension.

His mouth twisted in disgust. "That question doesn't deserve a reply, but since you obviously require one, let me tell you that we'd be finished if I wanted some other woman. As for ringing you, do you imagine that proves anything?" he mocked. "If I was that way inclined, I could just as easily cheat on the phone as I could any other way."

Lissa almost sagged with relief. What Kane said did make sense. His kind of sense. Kane Marriott always wanted the best. He would discard second-best on principle. A wave of pleasure followed the relief. For Kane, she was still the best. Nevertheless, he was not treating her right. Not by her lights.

"Why didn't you ring me?" she persisted stubbornly. "It would mean a lot to me if you did."

"Lissa, if you want a man on a string, find someone else. I'm no-one's puppet." He opened the passenger door, rounded the bonnet to the driver's side, unlocked that door and held it open for her. His eyes glittered with angry challenge. "Since you want to show me your driving skills, shall we get on with it?"

Lissa had never felt less like driving. Certainly there was no pleasure in it when the traffic was so heavy, and even less pleasure with Kane in a mood to criticise anything he would do better. But she had made a stand and she couldn't back down without looking like the petty kind of person Kane had accused her of being. She pushed her legs around the car, took the keys Kane held out to her and slid in behind the steering wheel. He closed the door on her with a firm snap.

Kane was not pleased by her behaviour tonight.

Lissa took a deep breath and released a long, shuddering sigh. She was not exactly pleased by his behaviour, either. Except . . . She lifted the posy of violets once more to her face, momentarily burying her nose in the intoxicating scent. Maybe he had bought these lovely flowers for her because she was the best woman for him. The best woman for sharing his bed, she reminded herself. As Kane dropped into the passenger seat beside her, she quickly twisted around to place the violets carefully on the back seat.

"No leg room in his car," he growled.

Her little Nissan was hardly in the same class as his Jaguar SL, but it served to get her around the city and Lissa was not about to apologise for it. "Use the lever under the seat to give yourself more room," she advised curtly, hoping he took the point that *he* was being unreasonable.

He did. Without further comment. She donned her seat belt and waited until he had fastened his, then concentrated on getting out of the car park without doing anything wrong. Once they were in the traffic stream that would take them into the city, she relaxed her concentration on driving to let her mind review the situation.

Kane hadn't offered a word since they had moved off. The tension in the car demolished any chance of easy conversation, yet Lissa had demanded this situation because she needed to talk to him. Now that she had him here with her, she realised that the answers she wanted were not the kind it was possible to get directly. The questions were almost impossible to ask. But she had to start somewhere.

"What do you want from this weekend, Kane?" she asked tentatively.

"You," he said.

"That's all?" she queried.

"God, Lissa!" he exploded irritably. "Don't you have any realisation that I shouldn't be here? I should be in Victoria, supervising what needs to be done. The only reason I'm here is because of you."

Which was immensely gratifying. Although she thought it unreasonable of him to expect her to realise such things when he didn't bother informing her of his work situation in any detail. However, she now knew he would be returning to Victoria after the weekend. Therefore this trip was out of the ordinary. She had never known Kane to leave anything until he was finished with it.

"You have a plan? A purpose? A strategy for this weekend?" she probed.

He slumped back in his seat and gave vent to a deep sigh. "I have a vision," he acknowledged wearily, "of what I want."

With Kane there was always a reason. Nothing happened for no reason at all. Lissa could not believe that his vision was centred on her. Only the top priority of his engineering company warranted a vision. She decided to probe a bit further.

"It's nice to know I mean something in your life," she said mockingly. "I would have thought the phone was easier."

"The satisfaction is not the same," he drawled.

Of course, she thought cynically. He couldn't have sex with her over the phone. "I guess if you don't have any other woman on the side, you need your R and R," she sniped.

That took the sardonic drawl out of his voice. "What do you mean by that?" he snarled.

"Isn't that what they say in the army? Rest and recreation?"

Irritation burst from him again. "Dammit, Lissa! Are you trying to spoil this before it starts?"

She exploded. "No, I'm not trying to spoil anything before it starts. I'm trying to get some answers. Like what I mean in your life!"

"I'm here, aren't I?" he grated.

"Yes," Lissa mocked. "You're here. Is it selfish here, because of your needs, or giving here, because of my needs?"

"Both."

No hesitation. Another concession of caring that she hadn't expected. It tapped into an uncontrollable well of hopeful feeling that had her hand reaching out, stroking down his thigh. She had always been a tactile person, instinctively translating emotion into touch.

She heard Kane's sharp intake of breath as the muscles in his thigh tightened to rock hardness. His hand clamped over hers, squeezed tight, halting its movement. "Concentrate on your driving, Lissa," he grated, then lifted her hand onto the steering wheel in an abrupt rejection of her caress.

"You're very tense," she commented, wishing she could read his mind.

"Extremely."

"Frustrated?"

"Intensely."

"Because of me or because of business?"

He gave a harsh little laugh. "Both."

She flicked a glance at him. He returned a crooked smile that mocked her concern. "I'll survive," he drawled. "I'm a specialist at surviving."

That was at least half the trouble with Kane, Lissa thought. His stone-hard self-sufficiency. Lissa suspected it was a direct by-product of his parents' divorce when he was twelve years old. The only kind of security he trusted was what he made for himself. At thirty-three, Kane was not about to change what had worked successfully for him. By *his* definition of success! Which had to do with being top dog of the territory he had carved out for himself.

She still didn't know where she fitted into his scheme of things. Most of Kane's personal relationships were tied in with his business world, and she doubted that any of them went deep. He had nothing to do with either of his parents, and although he had spoken of a younger sister whom he did visit occasionally, Lissa had never met her. Kane had never wanted to meet her family, either.

That was another source of her bitter discontent in her relationship with him. Lissa loved her family. They were an important part of her life. An integral part of her life. And Kane didn't want to recognise that, let alone accept it. He was bored by any talk of her parents or her three elder brothers. He listened, but she sensed he mentally switched off whenever she persisted with the subject. They were not people who counted for anything in his life.

The only member of her family he had met was the brother she shared an apartment with, and since Tony was a Qantas pilot and frequently away, their meetings had been brief, when Kane was either picking Lissa up for a weekend or dropping her home.

She knew her parents were hurt by the fact that she had never brought her boyfriend home to meet them, as she had always done before Kane. And she hated making excuses for him. Since they lived just outside the city at Berowra Waters, it was not as though they were a long way away. In fact, Lissa often drove to their home during the week for an overnight visit. Kane, however, was not inclined to share his time with Lissa with anyone else, unless the socialising was related to business.

Basically, he was a loner. Yet if he could be believed, he had stayed constant to her throughout their year-long relationship. She wondered if that was some kind of record for him. Then she recollected his comment that *he* would make up his mind this weekend about whether or not he wanted to continue their relationship. Was it about to come to an end no matter what she decided? That thought threw her into more emotional turmoil.

"When you return to Victoria, how long will you be away?" she asked.

It was an important question to her. She needed to know what to expect from him...*if* there was to be any future for them after this weekend.

Kane heaved another weary sigh. "God knows."

She darted a glance at him. He looked very tired. Strained and drained. "I miss you," she said softly, yearningly. She wanted him to ring her, to keep in touch, to share his life with her, to share her life with him.

Again the crooked smile. "I miss you a hell of a lot more."

It was a rare admission. Maybe Kane was softening. She flashed him a sympathetic smile. "Can't you get someone else to supervise the operation?"

"I will if I get the Wingicamble Project."

Lissa quickly switched her attention to the road. A hornet's nest of uncertainties buzzed through her mind as she recalled the decisions made at the board meeting this afternoon. Had Kane somehow known that his tenders were up for discussion today? Was that why he had come home, to pump her for information? Was she simply a double convenience to him, sex and business?

"I thought you had two tenders with ICAC," she said flatly, dying a little as she waited for him to pick up the lead-in.

"I have. If we get Jessamine, that will be cream on the cake. I *need* Wingicamble," he stated just as flatly.

She waited a few moments, but he didn't pursue the subject. Lissa's nerves throbbed with another thread of hope. Maybe their relationship did have priority for once. "Why is Wingicamble so important?" she asked.

"Because I'm living on the knife's edge. Without the ten-percent two-year retention rule, I'd be financially independent for life by now. That's all my profit. And I've got to wait two years for it. Without Wingicamble... Dammit! I need that cash flow to survive!"

Which explained why he was so tense. So irritable. And why she was taking second place in his life. Survival would always come first with Kane. But Lissa felt a lot better about that now. Particularly since he hadn't asked her about the tenders.

Maybe his life was dominated by the desire for money, prestige and success, the need to feed ego and self-esteem. But perhaps she was important in Kane's life, too. He had come home to be with her, and he had shown that he cared about her.

A new resolution blossomed in her mind. She would give him everything he wanted this weekend. Work at it. Give him the rest and recreation he obviously needed and wanted with her. Help him any way she could.

"Perhaps," she suggested tentatively, "if you're running your ship financially so close to the wind, you could try lowering your lifestyle. Don't spend so much on yourself."

"Don't try telling me how to run my business, Lissa," he said sharply. "What I spend on myself in one year wouldn't make a dent in my payroll tax, let alone a week's wages for the employees."

So much for being helpful, she thought. "I guess I'm out of my depth in your financial world."

"Yes, you are." Statement of fact. No compromise. Kane Marriott would always run his ship *his* way.

Lissa gave a sigh of wry resignation. "In that case, I suppose I can only give you..."

She couldn't find the heart to complete the sentence, but Kane knew straight away what she meant. He had the surrender he wanted. For this weekend.

He reached out and stroked her thigh. Whether it was a conciliatory gesture or a reclaiming of his possession, Lissa didn't know. The jolt of excitement at his provocative touch sent an involuntary spasm to her foot on the accelerator, and she almost rammed the car in front of her. Her heart bolted as she jerked her foot to the brake.

Having evaded disaster, she sucked in a deep breath and threw Kane a shaky look of reproach. "How can you expect me to concentrate on driving if you do that?"

"You always did have great reflexes," he said with a devilish grin that did nothing to calm her madly leaping pulse.

"Kane..."

The searing look in the dark eyes started an even faster drum roll through her heart. "Drive like the wind, Lissa," he said softly. "Blast through every hole in the traffic."

For the first time today, his voice had lost its edginess, the hard burr of a man who was being pushed to the limits. Lissa gave up on thinking. What would happen with Kane would happen. To her he had always been an irresistible force. Perhaps it was weak and stupid of her, but she would have this weekend with him anyway.

Whichever way she looked at it—loving him and wanting him as she did—it was still going to be one hell of a weekend...one way or another.

# CHAPTER FOUR

THE DRIVE to Kane's apartment in Woolhara was not a long one. Not only was it on the airport side of the city, but it could be reached through side streets, avoiding the congestion of main thoroughfares. It was not part of a big block of units, but an expensively renovated terrace house with its own small backyard and garage. This was reached by a narrow lane behind the row of terraces.

Kane opened the gate into the backyard for Lissa to park her car on the paving stones that covered most of the area. A profusion of tropical foliage down both side fences ensured privacy. Kane's choice of living quarters was typical of him. A class place in a class area, close and convenient to the centre of everything for business and entertainment purposes.

The house itself finished with a glassed-in conservatory, which was massed with ferns and orchids. Both the kitchen and the dining room faced onto this exotic view. Lissa and Kane walked through it to the sliding glass doors that led into the kitchen, a modern streamlined room, all white and stainless steel, extremely functional and always stocked with the makings for meals and drinks.

The decor of the apartment was ultra-modern; functional, luxurious and dramatic. The dining room and living room downstairs were furnished with leather, chrome and glass in a symphony of black and white and red, with a few dashes of green and purple for exotic effect. It screamed money from the soft wide lounges in the living room to the art-nouveau lamps and surrealist paintings on the walls. A wild, sensual decor in one respect, brashly new and simplistic in another. No frills. No harking back to a past that was meaningless to Kane. It was all here and now.

As Kane was here and now.

Complete unto himself.

Except, possibly, for Lissa.

A man as masculine as Kane needed a woman. The only question was, how much did he need *her* as opposed to any other woman? As they entered the kitchen, Lissa clutched the posy of violets with shaky tightness, almost as though it was a talisman.

"Your usual gin and tonic?" Kane asked, dumping his bags on the floor and moving straight to the refrigerator.

"Yes, thank you," she answered huskily, accepting there was no turning back now. The die was cast. The weekend had started.

*Drink, food, you....* That was the stated order of Kane's needs. She leaned against the sink, watching him as he dropped ice-cubes into glasses and poured the drinks. He enjoyed a gin and tonic, too, but obviously he needed a stronger slug of alcohol tonight.

He freely splashed Johnny Walker Swing over the ice in one of the glasses.

"Shall I defrost something?" she asked. It was a simple enough process with his computerised microwave oven. "What do you feel like eating?"

He gave her a look that was more eloquent than any words. He knew what he wanted to devour first. "Later," was all he said.

Lissa's skin began prickling with heat, her desire for him firing through her veins. She forced herself to move, to open the cupboard that stored a few vases. She did not want her violets to wilt for lack of water. For some reason it seemed important to keep them alive as long as she could.

She was heart-thumpingly aware of Kane shrugging off his leather jacket, tossing it onto a kitchen stool as she filled the vase with water. Out of the corner of her eye she saw him take a generous swig of whiskey, then carry both drinks towards her. He placed her gin and tonic on the sink beside her, his whiskey on the other side, his body trapping hers against the cupboard.

He moved provocatively against the soft curves of her bottom as she turned off the tap and set the vase aside. He spread his hands across her stomach, pressing her back against his rolling rhythm. He pushed her hair aside with his chin and trailed soft, burning kisses down her throat.

"I'm starved for the feel of you, the taste of you, the smell of you," he murmured, sweeping his mouth to her ear, licking its sensitive whirls with deft movements of his tongue.

"Kane . . . let me turn around," she gasped, jerking her head onto his shoulder to look at him, her eyes wide and appealing.

His were half-hooded but she glimpsed a taunting glitter as he moved his mouth over her cheek to her temples. The path of his lips left her skin tingling with excitement. She rubbed her hair against his shoulder, arched her neck as she let him find whatever targets he wanted to taste and tease, aware that he was not about to cede the control he was asserting until he was ready to. He slid a hand to the supple warmth of her breast. His fingers closed around it, exerting possessive and intensely sensual little pressures. A shaft of pure pleasure exploded through her stomach and spread to her thighs.

"I want you so badly," he said thickly.

"Let me kiss you, Kane," she pleaded, her voice husky with her yearning for him.

"Soon. I need to touch you all over. Make certain I haven't forgotten anything. I've missed you these last three weeks."

"I missed you, too," she protested.

"No other man, Lissa?"

"No."

"No *perhaps?*"

She shook her head, unable to speak as his mouth closed over the throbbing arteries in her neck with intense passion. It seemed that he wanted to draw on her lifeblood or revel in its wildly pulsating response to his fierce hunger for her.

Lissa swayed against him, inviting the tightening of his arms around her, savouring his strength and his need as he pressed her closer to him, his hands moving restlessly, yearningly over the swelling sensitivity of her breasts.

His lips trailed hotly to her ear. "Don't ever suggest any other man. Ever again!" he commanded, a harsh possessiveness in his voice.

"I won't," she promised.

He slid his hands to her thighs, stroking a compelling awareness of her femininity, of her need as a woman. She could feel the strength and power of his desire and moved her body sinuously to provoke him. A hissed intake of breath was his only reaction.

His determination to retain control seeded the thought that he wanted to possess her mind as well as her body, to own her completely, to drive her mad for him, to stamp his touch on her so she would never forget it. And never again think of any other man!

If he really cared about her enough to stay constant all this time, she had hurt him by putting that uncertainty into his mind this morning.

"I didn't mean what I said on the phone, Kane," she said regretfully. "I was angry with you. Because you hadn't called."

"My little she-cat," he drawled in his velvet voice with all its dangerous undertones. He twirled her around in his arms, and there was a devilish curl on his lips, a raw blaze of passion in his eyes. "Needs to be taught not to play with fire," he finished mockingly.

"I wanted some part of you, Kane. That's all," she explained. "I felt . . . deprived."

"So did I. Very deprived."

He tilted her chin. His eyes glittered into hers, challenging her to deny him what he was intent on taking. She had aroused the devil in him, Lissa realised. He intended to possess her tonight. Totally. The thought both repelled and excited her. He was very much a male animal, growling over his territory, asserting his ownership, and despite all her uncertainties about him, there was a deeply primitive part of her that was uncontrollably stirred by Kane Marriott's aggressive sexuality.

His mouth covered hers, hungry and urgent, yet still he held enough control to subtly persuade her lips apart with the tip of his tongue before sweeping quickly within to trace those sensitive areas that fired her blood with the wild response he could always evoke. The kiss deepened, quickened, whirled out of control on a surging current of frantic desire. Lissa's fingers raked through the silky thickness of his hair, clutching, clinging. She felt Kane's hands circling the soft underswell of her breasts, lifting their fullness into firmer contact with his hard chest. Her body was turning to yearning jelly for him to mould as he pleased.

Strong, raking fingers gathered the soft woollen fabric of her skirt. She could feel the hardness of his arousal pressed against the silk camisole that covered her stomach. His hands moved to her tights. He tore the thin nylon asunder. Lissa jerked her head back, her eyes flying open in shocked realisation of what he intended as he moved her panties aside.

"Not here, Kane," she choked out.

Black unfathomable need swirled down at her.

"Yes," he rasped.

She felt his naked flesh come against her, rigid and unyielding. Her muscles tightened with shock, but a persuasive caress of his hands shattered her initial reaction.

"Here," he said, "and now!" A deep satisfaction glittered over his need.

She was beyond protesting as his hands curled around her buttocks and lifted her against the kitchen sink. His hot, throbbing flesh entered her with plunging urgency. One arm held her pinned to him as his other hand entwined itself in her hair, arching her body for his mouth to ravish hers in a devastating reinforcement of his possession. Lissa was helpless against the sensations that stormed through her in overwhelming waves. She melted around him, his short, masterful stroking too compelling to deny.

Why do I love him, she thought. Why? Why? Why? There has to be more to love than this fiercely primitive coupling. Yet she didn't stop her legs from winding around his thighs, holding him fast to the inner world they shared. Nor could she deny the mad exultation that coursed through her as she felt the explosion of his apocalyptic orgasm.

All thought fractured into meaningless drifts across her mind as Kane kept moving inside her, savouring her, as Lissa savoured him, the feeling of relief and release lingering on, too sweet to let go. She loved these precious moments with him. More than any other. He held her with such heart-melting gentleness, soothing, protective. For a long time she had thought it was love, but she knew better now. Kane was a good lover who would treat any woman the same way.

He rubbed his cheek over her hair as she rested her head on his shoulder. He was such a complex mixture of harsh ruthlessness and sensitive tenderness, she thought, and wished she could understand him and the forces that made him what he was.

"I guess I should never talk about other men," she said dreamily, "if this is what happens."

"I wouldn't make a habit of it," he agreed, his voice a low gravelly throb, as though her comment hit on a painful area that threatened to flare up again, given the slightest provocation.

Maybe he cares a lot more about me than I think he does, Lissa mused hopefully. Or maybe it's just a possessive thing. No point in hiding her head on his shoulder any more, she mocked herself. Yet she lifted it reluctantly, not sure that she wanted to see what was in his eyes. Although if they showed her anything of his inner feelings, she wanted to know. He looked at her with soft mockery, hot chocolate, no sugar.

She stroked a finger down his cheek. "Happy now?" she probed lightly.

"Almost."

Kane was definitely not the greatest communicator in the world. Certainly not verbally. Not with her, anyway. "What more do you want?" she asked.

"I'll show you."

He carried her up to his bedroom, undressed her and made love to her. Slowly this time. A totally different kind of possession. More thorough in its attention to every part of her, more pervasive in its intoxicating sensuality, more intent on giving and taking every possible nuance of pleasure. Wanting everything.

He *was* frustrated—very frustrated, Lissa thought. He couldn't have been having any other woman on the side. She *was* the only one in his life. If only Kane could be more concerned and caring beyond this physical expression, which had to be almost an art form of loving, she would be so happy with him. As blissfully content as he was making her feel now with the power he unharnessed from his body, suffusing hers with it, inside and out, enclosing her in a capsule of pulsing life that was uniquely theirs.

She loved his body, loved feeling the ripple of muscle under his firm flesh, loved the look of him, so strong and magnificently proportioned, loved the touch of his satin-smooth skin and the contrasting roughness of the springy hair that furred the sensitive area below his throat and the long, powerful legs. To lie entwined with him in the long, languorous aftermath of loving was exquisite pleasure to Lissa.

Eventually Kane rolled onto his back, carrying her with him so that she lay half-sprawled across his chest. He stroked her hair as though she was the she-cat he had called her, his personal pet who gave him tactile satisfaction over and above the easing of the tensions that built up inside him.

Perhaps she was special to him, but he didn't say, "I love you." Lissa wondered if it was because he was totally honest and couldn't bring himself to say something he didn't mean, or if he was incapable of saying something that revealed any deep vulnerability, or perhaps his past had made him incapable of loving anyone.

She hitched herself up, wanting to see what was written on his face. If his guard was down for once. There was a relaxed softness that made him seem more approachable than usual. His dark eyes met hers, not quite openly, but with a glow of warm pleasure that told her he was momentarily satisfied with what they had shared.

She traced his lips with a feather-light finger. "I thought the agenda was drink first, food second and this third," she said, seeking an admission that would satisfy the deep craving in her heart.

"I had a drink," he said defensively.

"One mouthful," she reminded him.

"That was enough."

"What about the food?" she persisted, wanting him to say what she needed to hear.

He playfully bit her finger, then gave her a slow, satisfied smile. "Sometimes priorities have to be changed."

She smiled with a touch of irony. "Your priority changes are fairly predictable, Kane."

He arched an eyebrow at her. "Are you complaining, Lissa?"

"No." She sighed. How could she complain about a touch of artistry that could transport her beyond all hard realities?

Perhaps some of her painful vulnerability to those hard realities swam into her eyes. His focus seemed to sharpen to an intense watchfulness. "What would you say if I said I loved you, Lissa?" he asked softly.

Her heart turned over. She looked at him with both suspicion and hope. Suspicion won. There was a reason behind everything Kane said. He was speaking from his head, not his heart, probably seeking some lever to keep their relationship going as he wanted it.

Kane had never loved anything or anybody in his life. He hated his mother for her selfish pursuit of her own gratifications. He hated his father for not fighting for what was his, for weakly accepting what his wife had done to him and their children. He hated his sister's neurotic dependence on other people and things, although he did hold some grudging affection for her. If loving had ever been in his nature, Kane had stamped it out as something too unreliable to trust.

"I'd say you were lying," she replied with a mocking little grimace that she hoped hid the pain behind the words.

"Why?"

"Oh, an hour ago you were pointing to the airport terminal exit and saying that was the way out of your life," she drawled in a pointed reminder of his callous bluntness.

"I was giving you a choice."

"It didn't exactly fill me with confidence about how much you love me, Kane."

His mouth twisted. "You gave me the same feeling with your suggestions on the phone."

That had certainly cut deep. Lissa considered the implications. Was it pride in his manhood that had been wounded, pride spurring him to prompt her into a declaration of love for him? She had definitely threatened his sense of security with her suggestion of interest in another man. Would only absolute possession of her—mind and heart and soul—satisfy Kane now?

All so one-sided, she thought despondently. Kane didn't love her. He wouldn't treat her so cavalierly if he loved her. This was a power game, and he was testing to see how much power he had over her. Not this weekend, she silently promised him. This weekend we meet head to head, Kane Marriott.

She shrugged. "Perhaps we're no good for each other."

His fingers feathered down her spine, making her shiver with pleasure. He smiled. "You can say that now?" he taunted softly.

She bridled at his confidence in his ability to please her on a physical level. "I said I'll make up my mind on Sunday night, Kane."

The glitter of challenge sharpened his eyes to a searing brilliance. "About being in love?"

She deliberately kept her expression bland, revealing none of her emotional torment. "About staying with you. For a while longer."

"While it suits you."

Again she shrugged. "Something like that."

"And if I said I don't love you?" he posed derisively.

"I'd believe you."

He laughed. But not with his eyes. "Do you know what love is, Lissa?"

"Do you, Kane?" she challenged with arch scepticism.

His mouth curled sardonically. "I guess not."

He guessed right, Lissa thought with bitter cynicism. She was a weak, stupid fool for capitulating to him about the weekend. But being with him like this, she couldn't honestly regret it. Not yet. And since he had opened up areas that had been avoided before tonight, Lissa decided now was as good a time as any to find out how she really stood with him.

"If you had to choose between me and your business, what would you choose, Kane?"

He shrugged. "It's a hypothetical question. It would never happen."

Ever the realist, Lissa thought. Nothing the least bit sentimental about Kane. It was truly a marvel that he had actually thought to buy her the posy of violets. "But what would you choose?" she insisted, intent on forcing an answer.

"At the present moment?"

If she had ever had a correct moment, it was now when she had satisfied his needs. "Yes," she said. "Right at this present moment."

There was not the slightest flicker of uncertainty. He looked at her squarely and said, "I'd choose the business."

Totally honest, totally ruthless Kane. So much for love! She had known that, of course, but the hurt was still deeply wounding.

"Any particular reason?" she asked, pretending a curious interest.

"It's more predictable," he answered nonchalantly.

"Is that all?"

With a flash of hot savagery, he turned her onto her back, leaning over her with an air of barely repressed violence. "This morning you told me you were leaving me. Finis. Not even a fare thee well," he snarled.

Lissa stared at him, astonished more than alarmed by the abrupt change of mood. Her defection had stirred deeper and darker passions inside Kane than she had ever imagined it would. "Only because you are what you are," she defended hotly.

"Which is what?"

"Uncaring and uncompromising about everything but your own needs."

He smoothly mended the crack in his formidable control, raising his eyebrows in arrogant contempt for her contentions. "Absurd," he drawled.

"It's not absurd," she snapped at him. "It only takes small gestures—"

"Like using the phone?" he scoffed.

"Exactly," she bit out angrily.

A bitter cynicism glinted in his eyes. "And giving you flowers?"

"It all helps," she insisted, fiercely resenting his dismissal of things that meant a lot to her.

"And you call that love, Lissa?" Incredulity shaded the dangerous tone in his soft voice.

Her strongly held beliefs denied any room for doubt. "Gestures like that show that you're not thinking entirely of yourself all the time. They show you care! And without caring, there is no love."

His face hardened. "What do you want me to do? Bring you a cup of coffee in bed every morning?"

"That sounds like a fine idea!"

"If you want the kind of nursemaid my sister has for a husband, you'd better look elsewhere. That's not my idea of love," he stated bitingly.

"I didn't think it would be, Kane," she mocked. "You never give an inch."

His eyes shone jet black, his inner self totally closed off from her. "I can see this is going to be one hell of a weekend."

"That's what I thought," she agreed, savagely denying the awful quiver in her heart. "Maybe it's best if I go now. After all, your frustration is somewhat relieved," she added with acid sarcasm.

He gave a harsh little laugh. "You think so, do you, Lissa? You think all I need from you is a sexual fix? You think that's what keeps me coming back to you? Your delectable body?"

Yes, it was what she thought, but it was too demeaning to admit it. The violence of her feelings turned love to hatred as he deliberately ran his hand down her body in an insidious caress that still had the power to make her flesh leap with excitement.

The black eyes burned into hers with all the knowledge of the intimacies she had let him take...that he was still taking. "Let me tell you, Lissa," he said softly, "there is no arrangement of female flesh that could hold me. Or keep me coming back to it. However beautiful. And you are very beautiful. As exquisitely feminine as any man could desire."

"Then what does keep you coming back to me?" she asked shakily, her emotions in upheaval.

His mouth twisted into a derisive little smile. "Would you believe...your sweet, giving nature?"

She caught his hand as it glided towards the sweetness he could so knowingly arouse. "I give in to what you want, you mean," she interpreted bitterly.

His lips thinned into a hard straight line. His eyes glittered in angry challenge. "*Give in,* Lissa? Are you implying that the pleasure we have in each other is not mutual?"

She flushed, unable to deny that she was willing, had always been willing, was more than willing to share this physical intimacy with him. But it wasn't enough. It would never be enough for her.

"It's mutual," she acknowledged, her eyes flashing dark purple with resentment. "But you make me feel I'm only a sex object to you."

His face tightened as though she had hit him. He instantly withdrew his hand from under hers. "I would never, ever consider any woman as a sex object," he bit out, his eyes searing hers with an icy fire that left her in total confusion. "I was cured of strictly carnal desires a long time ago," he added with intense bitterness.

He rolled off the bed onto his feet and was striding for the built-in wardrobe before Lissa could recover any equilibrium at all. Somehow her words had evoked dark memories that spurred more than a merely physical withdrawal from her. The chill of rejection started creeping through her bones. Yet surely she had been justified in saying what she had.

"Where are you going?" she asked, unsure whether he meant to refrain from any further lovemaking with her. Unsure what he meant about anything, where she was concerned. Except that his business came first.

"To get some food," he replied brusquely, not bothering to glance at her as he opened a cupboard door and drew out the black towelling bathrobe he favoured.

Lissa sighed, far from satisfied with that reply. "I suppose you want me to cook something," she said dully.

He thrust his arms into the sleeves and turned to face her as he wrapped the loose edges across each other and tied the belt. His handsome face had tightened into hard angles. The black eyes were savagely mocking.

"I thought, by your definition, that was the action of someone in love," he drawled.

"I never said I loved you," she defended, denying him that power over her. He had too much as it was.

"I can see that," he mocked. "So I'll cook the damned stuff myself."

"You've got an intolerable temper," she hurled after him as he strode for the door.

He paused, stabbed a blazing look at her. "But we are good for some things together, aren't we, Lissa?" he fired, then walked out on that undeniable exit line.

Lissa burned for several minutes, silently railing over how impossible Kane Marriott was. He could insist in one breath that she wasn't and never had been a sex object to him. Then in the next breath, he was reminding her what was good between them. He was an infuriating enigma, and she would never understand him as long as she lived.

No doubt about it.

With their relationship splintered by all this sniping bitchery, it was most definitely going to be a very, very long weekend!

# CHAPTER FIVE

LISSA DRAGGED HERSELF off the bed. She grimaced at her reflection in the mirrored doors of the built-in wardrobe. *Beautiful and exquisitely feminine?* Well, she certainly didn't look boyish, she thought wryly. She wondered if Kane would have bothered taking a second look at her if she wasn't built the way she was.

Kane might not think he considered her a sex object, but that was how he used her. She suited his bedroom very well. At least her colouring did, she thought ruefully, eyeing the reflection of the bed in the mirrored doors.

Red satin sheets and pillowslips. A quilt cover made from a brilliant Jenny Kee original print, which was a complex design in deep sea green, vivid acid yellow, lime green, violet, purple, blue... and red. The deep green carpet was the perfect foil for it. The sound system had black speakers, and the space-age Sony Trinitron TV was also black. So were the expensively lacquered bedside tables.

Lissa heaved a deep sigh. One thing could be said for Kane. There was nothing wishy-washy about him. Not in his decision-making, nor in his taste in decor. His electric vitality *touched* everything. And for all his shortcomings, Lissa had to admit she felt more vibrantly alive with him than at any other time of her life, or with anyone else. She picked up her mauve silk-and-lace camisole from the floor and slipped it over her head. No point in staying in Kane's bedroom when he wasn't there.

He didn't hear her come downstairs. The thick carpet underfoot muffled any sound of her approach. Lissa paused in the doorway between the dining room and the kitchen and watched him, trying to see beyond his ill humour to the man inside.

He slammed the freezer shut, dumped a couple of frozen steaks on the sink, moved to the refrigerator, opened the door, bent down to the vegetable crisper, took out some onions, kicked the drawer shut with his foot, kicked the refrigerator door shut, tossed the onions into the sink. It was Kane's habit to peel onions under water.

Every action denoted tension. If sex had been meant to relax him, it hadn't worked. Or only momentarily. Besides which, things weren't going all his way this weekend. It was clear that he wanted his sweet, soft, darling Lissa back, not a shrew who was spoiling everything.

He looked very tired. The skin around his eyes was drawn, and the lines on either side of his mouth seemed more deeply grooved than usual. Kane did work hard. He gave almost all of himself to his business, and undoubtedly the last three weeks had taken a heavy toll on him. He couldn't possibly feel like cooking a meal. Only extreme hunger or perverse pride was making him do it. Or to show her up. Probably all three.

"Will a steak do, or shall I get something else for you?" he asked carelessly.

Lissa couldn't bear this kind of attitude. Perhaps she should go now, she thought, but she had given her word to spend the weekend with him, and somehow it was a matter of pride not to back out of it at this point.

"Why don't we go to Lucio's?" she suggested. "It's only a few blocks. And you always like the food there."

It was his favorite Italian restaurant. Maybe they could both relax a little over a fine meal and a bottle of wine. The walk in the cool night air might iron out some of their tension, as well. To her intense relief the idea found favour with Kane.

"We'll have to dress again," he remarked, his face slowly softening into a rueful little smile.

"I don't mind if you don't," Lissa said agreeably.

"I don't think your tights are wearable."

She shrugged. "I don't need them."

"I can't seem to curb my impetuosity today."

The wry remark made her smile. "I've been a little on edge myself," she said apologetically, wanting the bickering ended. It wasn't serving any purpose. Kane was Kane. He wasn't going to change because she wanted him to. He had spelled that out only too clearly.

He crossed the kitchen, slid his arms around her, drew her into an undemanding embrace, then kissed her with a sweet tenderness that turned her heart over. "Truce?" he asked whimsically, the dark eyes twinkling an appeal.

"Truce," she agreed.

He stroked her cheek, searched her eyes in a wondering fashion, then decisively turned aside to use the telephone. "I'll ring Lucio's and see if they have a table," he said.

"Whatever you like," Lissa answered carelessly.

She had spotted her posy of violets lying on the side of the sink. She had filled a vase with water, but Kane had distracted her from putting the flowers into it. As he dialled the number for the restaurant, she moved across to rectify the matter.

She knew Kane turned to watch her, but she didn't care how little he thought of his gift of flowers. She loved it. Her hand automatically lifted the posy to her nose to sniff the scent again before carefully lowering the stems into the vase of water. Later, she promised herself, she would carry the vase upstairs and set it on one of the bedside tables. Then she could look at the flowers while Kane made love to her and pretend that they were a gift of love. Foolish, perhaps, but what harm was there in a little pretence this last weekend? She would have to face reality soon enough. Couldn't there be some sweetness with all the bitterness?

She heard Kane hang up the telephone and glanced inquiringly at him. He was looking at her with a quizzical expression on his face, as though meditating on something he had never thought about before.

"Is it all right?" she asked.

"Mmm . . . they'll hold a table for us." He nodded towards the vase. "The flowers really please you, Lissa?"

She returned her own puzzlement at his curious question. "Didn't you think they would, Kane?"

He gave an offhand shrug. "I guess I don't tend to think along those lines. I find it . . . artificial."

"Why?"

His face hardened. "Nobody ever did anything for me that didn't have a price-tag on it."

Poor Kane. Unloved and unloving. *Nobody ever did anything for me.* People looked up to him, seeing the success he was, not realising the cost, the bitter dark void in his soul, his isolation from the rest of humanity. He *needed* someone to care for him. For himself. Not his position, not his wealth. For the boy he had been, unwanted and unloved. She moved towards him spontaneously, starting to understand.

She suddenly realised why he had begrudged giving her the posy. He considered it dishonest to have to buy affection. The revelation gave her a valuable insight into how Kane thought about people. It also undermined several of her resentments.

"It's not the cost. It's the thought—the gesture—that counts," she tried to explain, wanting him to understand, realising that he could not have had the example of a loving and caring family life that had patterned her thinking.

In a way, she supposed she had been spoiled by all the little attentions given her by her parents and brothers—the only daughter, the little sister, dearly loved. She had sorely missed that kind of indulgence from Kane. In a type of perverse pride, she had withheld from him what he had withheld from her, and she saw now how wrong that had been of her. He didn't know any better, but she did.

"You don't have to buy anything, Kane," she continued softly. "If you stopped your car by the roadside and picked a few wild flowers because you were thinking of me and thought I might like them, I'd be just as pleased. It's doing things that show you care."

Her mouth twisted with irony. "Like three weeks of silence shows that you don't care. At least, that's what it seems like to me." Her eyes begged the truth from him. "Am I wrong about that, Kane?"

He didn't snap irritably this time. He took a few moments to consider what she had said, and finally conceded more than he had ever conceded before. "I do think of you, Lissa. More than I want to."

Another revealing little comment! He obviously didn't like not being able to completely control the part she played in his life. "Is it so painful?" she asked.

"It can be."

The terse little reply indicated his displeasure at having been constrained to do more than he usually did in order to have her this weekend.

"You haven't had much practice at loving, have you, Kane?"

"Not a lot," he acknowledged mockingly.

Lissa persisted. "Why not try it sometimes? Just for a change?"

"It shows weakness. A lack of independence."

"You can't bear that?"

A grim, humourless smile. "Let's say I'm wary of giving anyone an advantage that can be used against me."

Proud, independent, untouchable Kane.

Yet surely no man was an island. Not completely. However repressed it was, there was that spark of humanity in everyone that wanted to reach out, to be known and understood and cared about by at least one other person. Perhaps it was Lissa he wanted to reach, but he couldn't quite let himself go, because if she let him down he would hate himself for having been so weak as to admit her past his self-protective defences.

"You don't concede much, Kane," she said quietly.

"Neither do you, Lissa."

She shook her head in painful bemusement. It was he who set the barriers, she who beat her head and heart against them. To her way of thinking, she had given herself to him totally. That was why his long silences were intolerable. Yet clearly he felt she failed him in some way. In his mind, she had certainly failed him this morning when she had stopped conceding to *his* plans.

"I guess you get hard... when you have to fight hardness," she said flatly.

Her eyes dropped from his and fastened on the violets again. They were proof that he had thought of her at the airport after she had raised uncertainties about this weekend. Given his beliefs, he had bought them cynically, in an attempt to buy her compliance. At least he hadn't been so cynical as to buy red roses. Too honest for that. But ruthless enough to do whatever he thought he had to do to get what he wanted. And he did still want her. As much as he ever had. That hadn't waned at all. It seemed to have intensified under the threat of her leaving him.

"Would it help if I show what I did think about you while I was in Victoria?"

She dragged her gaze off the violets and looked at him with dull, sceptical eyes. "How are you going to do that, Kane?"

There was a black determination in his eyes, hard purpose carved on his face. Lissa had the forceful impression that Kane had made up his mind to take a chance, but he had himself steeled against a negative result.

He made no verbal reply to her question. He walked over to the bags he had dropped earlier, picked up his attaché case, which carried all his business papers, picked up his suitcase, as well. "Wait here," he said.

He'd left his keys upstairs, of course. "I might as well come with you."

He cocked a mocking eyebrow at her. "Impatient?"

"Practical."

He shrugged. "If you must."

"I have to dress if we're going out, and my clothes are in your bedroom," Lissa reminded him pointedly.

"True," he conceded, and waved her ahead of him.

In truth, she had no expectations. The fact that Kane had gone straight to his attaché case indicated that what he had in mind was related to his business in some way. He had probably thought of something he could use as a conciliatory gesture. A bolster to his truce for the weekend. At least he was trying, Lissa thought, which was a bit of a change. Although it obviously went against his grain.

When they reached the bedroom, Lissa started picking up her clothes, not bothering to watch what Kane was doing. Expecting anything from Kane Marriott—apart from what came within his rules for a relationship—was pure self-delusion.

"Lissa?"

She looked up at the impatient note in his voice.

"Don't you want to see?" he asked.

"You said you'd show me."

"So I did," he said in dry acknowledgment. "Leave that. Turn around and face the mirror. And hold up your hair."

She frowned at him, all her preconceptions confused by the instruction. She slowly did as she was told, thinking he must have bought her a necklace of some kind. Nothing else seemed to make sense. Maybe a gold chain, she thought. That made sense.

But what he hung around her neck was nothing like anything she would ever expect Kane to choose. It was an amethyst pendant, set in a delicately crafted and rather old-fashioned design of gold filigree and seed pearls. It was not flashy. Not dramatic. Not wildly exotic. It was beautiful. And exquisitely feminine.

"You can let your hair down now," he instructed.

She dropped her arm in a daze of disbelief and heart-squeezing delight. He fluffed out the blue-black mass of waves and curls around her shoulders, then adjusted the position of the amethyst to his liking.

"It looked at me and said Lissa. Don't ask me why," he added in a terse rasp. "I felt like buying it for you. So I did."

He took his hand away from the pendant and lightly grasped her upper arms. The dark eyes sought hers in the mirror, looking for her reaction. "Do you like it, Lissa?" he asked gruffly.

Tears welled into her eyes. She couldn't help it. Impossible to speak. Her throat was choked by a huge lump of emotion. The violets, now this.... It was so special, especially chosen for her because this was how he thought of her.... And she had been so wrong, so terribly wrong, so wonderfully wrong, because maybe Kane did love her in his way.

The tears overflowed and trickled through her thick lashes. She bit her lip, tried to swallow, blinked hard. But the tears kept filling her eyes as she stared and stared at Kane's surprise. Her heart squeezed tighter and tighter.

"Lissa?" Kane's face was blurred, but she heard the strained uncertainty in his voice. He gently turned her around and wrapped her in his arms. "Why are you crying, Lissa?"

She had never done it before. Not with Kane. No matter how hurt she had felt at times, pride had demanded that she hold a strong, hard front because he was so hard and strong. But his gift, and now his gentleness, somehow undermined all the defences she had built, and the truth came blurting out.

"I thought... I thought you picked me up and put me down at your convenience. And you never thought of me in between."

He rubbed his cheek over her hair and stroked her back with slow, rhythmic, soothing caresses as she soaked the shoulder of his bathrobe. What he thought she didn't know. He said nothing. It didn't seem to matter. He held her as she needed to be held, with every semblance of loving tenderness.

The intense wave of emotion eventually drained away. Lissa took several deep breaths and managed enough composure to bring herself to look at Kane. His face looked grim. He returned her troubled gaze, his eyes reflecting a dark inner turbulence. She wondered if she had stirred a feeling of something that he didn't like or want. To be wrong about anything would not sit well with Kane.

"I'm sorry," she said impulsively, not wanting him to feel bad when he had made her feel good. "Thank you, Kane."

She reached up to kiss him. His lips were stiff, unresponsive at first. Then his arms tightened around her and his mouth started to move urgently over hers, hungry with pent-up feelings that suddenly exploded into fierce passion.

It was just as well she hadn't bothered with dressing, Lissa reflected afterwards, or Kane might have torn everything she was wearing. Not that she would have minded. There had been a totally uncontrolled quality about Kane's lovemaking this time, which she found deeply satisfying. As though he couldn't help himself. Which had never happened before. A lot of firsts this weekend, she thought, and it had barely begun. Where it would end, she no longer knew. But the empty black void had moved farther away.

"We definitely need food," Kane declared on a long sigh.

"Yes," Lissa agreed. "If you're going to keep this pace up...."

He laughed and scooped her off the bed with him as he swung his feet to the floor and stood up. "We'll have a quick shower together. Save time."

"You like touching me, you mean," she teased.

He grinned at her. "You know me so well."

"Maybe not so well as I thought. But some things are very predictable."

He cocked a wicked eyebrow at her. "You prefer not to be soaped all over?"

She laughed and bit his shoulder. "I love to be soaped all over."

"I don't mind what you do to me, either."

It was almost another hour before they set out for Lucio's. Kane said it didn't matter. He held Lissa's hand as they walked along. Occasionally she lifted her other hand to touch the amethyst pendant. It was the middle of winter, and the night air was particularly crisp after the warmth of the apartment, but it made Lissa's senses feel even more vibrantly alive.

It was a beautiful night. The stars were out. A light breeze rustled the leaves in the trees along the footpath. Kane was beside her.

This wasn't going to be one hell of a weekend after all, Lissa thought blissfully. This was going to be the best weekend of her life.

# CHAPTER SIX

LUCIO'S WAS A TERRACE house, renovated to suit the needs of a restaurant. It had two dining rooms, and in summer a third was added by using the garden at the back. The decor was unpretentious and rather Spartan—pink tablecloths, pink walls, undressed windows that overlooked the street—and background music was unobtrusively played. The waiters were friendly and caring, the service very good, the ambience excellent and the food superb. It was a pleasant place to be.

Lissa and Kane were welcomed at the door and escorted to the only vacant table left in the front room. There was a break in the buzz of conversation as they were seated. Kane was well-known here and something of a minor celebrity since he had been connected to the construction of quite a few large public projects. He always drew women's eyes, and men looked at him with curiosity, envy and respect.

If Kane noticed at all, he never let it touch him. Lissa, however, was always conscious of the way women looked him over. At first, it had made her feel insecure, and it had contributed to her giving in to Kane's rules, because she was only too aware that if she didn't please him, some other woman was only too ready to do so. In that sense, Lissa realised, she had made her own problems with Kane, repressing what should not have been repressed, bottling up her resentments until they had come to a head this weekend.

She had instigated a few minor confrontations along the way, but she had always been the one to back down, to let the issues slide rather than force them. She had seen no other option if she wanted to keep him. Kane Marriott did not bend. Nor could he be persuaded. He decided. And that was that.

Until today.

Something was different. She could feel it in her blood. Although it wasn't that Kane was any less decisive. He was simply making decisions she had never expected him to make. It was only now, when he had unequivocally told her she was the only woman he wanted in his life—and in his own way had proved it to her—that Lissa could finally acknowledge that Kane was not a woman hunter and seducer. In fact, to her recollection, he had never looked speculatively at another woman since he had met her.

Nor did he now. As far as he was concerned, Lissa was the only woman in the restaurant. He sat opposite her, and apart from discussing their meal order with their waiter, he gave her all his attention. His eyes played continually over her face. His mouth was ready to smile at anything she said. His whole expression was one of warm pleasure in being with her. Lissa could feel her face glowing with the happiness inside her.

They started with a plate of antipasto and a bottle of Lungarotti San Giorgio. As usual, everything was delicately prepared and delicious. To her surprise, Lissa found she had a hearty appetite. It had been a long time since lunch, but with her churning stomach, she hadn't felt like food at all. It must have been the expenditure of energy since Kane had come home, she decided. Her body was crying out for sustenance.

"How was the food in Victoria?" she asked.

"I didn't notice. It was food. That's all."

Fuel to keep going, he meant. Business had his total concentration. Lissa could well imagine him not noticing anything else.

"Are the main problems at the construction site sorted out now?"

"The worst of it is over. It will take a bit more riding." There was a brief flash of contempt. "Too many people wanting to compromise. That's not the way to get things done."

Not Kane's way, Lissa thought. Not anyone's way, she corrected herself. Not if they wanted to be successful. Lissa did appreciate that from her daily contact with Jack Conway. If a delivery schedule looked like going over contract, it not only jeopardised profits, it jeopardised the jobs of the employees. Profits paid wages. So there was certainly a time and place to be ruthless.

The trouble with Kane was the way he carried it over into his personal life. On the other hand, Lissa mused, perhaps that kind of capability only came from a man who had it ingrained in his nature.

She wondered what Jack Conway was like in his personal life. All she knew was that he had stayed married to the same woman for thirty years. She was quite sure, however, that if he had played around, he had never put his priorities at risk. Divorce, she had heard him argue, was financially stupid. It was a loss of assets. Jack Conway didn't believe in losing assets. Lissa imagined that Kane would probably feel the same way. Financial considerations would always rule Kane's world.

No, that wasn't the only consideration, Lissa swiftly reminded herself. For Kane Marriott, there would be more to keeping a marriage going than retaining assets. He was the product of a broken marriage. He hated divorce. Bitterly. So much of what he had become was a direct result of what had happened between his father and mother. Lissa was sure of it.

While he never elaborated on his personal experience, from the few acid comments he had made from time to time, Lissa could guess it had been an extremely traumatic period in his life. And his younger sister's. Kane would never inflict that kind of mental and emotional torment on his children if he married. His commitment would be rock solid.

She wondered if being cured of carnal desires related to that time. She wished he would talk openly about it.

"What are you thinking?" Kane asked suddenly, a curious glint in his eyes.

Lissa hesitated. This was sensitive ground. And intrusive. "What you said about not considering any woman a sex object," she said slowly.

"Do you consider any man a sex object?" he teased. His brilliant dark eyes sparkled with warm indulgence.

"Some men look more attractive than others," she mused. Kane certainly did. "But I agree with you. That's not what holds you."

"What holds you to me, Lissa?" Kane asked softly.

The directness of the question startled her. It was not like Kane to probe personal feelings. Although he had done it earlier tonight when he had brought up the subject of love. She thought about it for several moments.

"Do you want the truth?" she asked ruefully.

"Yes."

She sighed. Her hands fluttered in a little gesture of appeal and apology for her inability to give concrete reasons. "I guess the closest I can come to describing it is that I feel more of everything when I'm with you. Life is sharper, brighter, darker...." Her mouth twisted self-mockingly. "And when you're away I only feel half-live."

He frowned, nodded thoughtfully, then shot her a look of understanding. "That's why you want me to telephone you. To keep the feeling going."

"One reason," she acknowledged.

"I'll do it in future, Lissa," he decided.

She shook her head incredulously. Decision made. Just like that. Then she realised Kane had changed his perceptions of her needs. He no longer thought she wanted him as a puppet on a string.

"What holds you to me?" she asked, wondering if he would give her any other answer besides, "Being good together."

He gave her his crooked smile. "I guess it's something similar." The smile faded. The dark eyes gathered a sharp intensity. Then he softly added, "I know I want to keep you, Lissa. How do you feel about that?"

Keep? As a convenient tumble in bed whenever he wanted her? A continuation of meeting for weekends with no more than being good together? Plus the occasional phone call he had conceded? Lissa's heart fluttered between hope and despair. She wanted so much more from Kane than he gave her, but he was starting to give. With more time, and more understanding between them, perhaps they might come to the kind of sharing that meant they answered each other's needs.

"I'm not sure I know specifically what you mean, Kane," she answered doubtfully. "What do you have in mind? What are you looking for?"

"Marriage."

That one word stole Lissa's breath and shook her to her toes. She stared at him in shock. Her heart catapulted all around her chest. Was he serious?

He reached across the table, took her hands. His face was sternly set. His eyes were black, impenetrable, focused with deep, unknown intent upon her. "I'm asking you to marry me, Lissa," he said.

"You can't be serious," she croaked, her mouth dry, her throat dry, her whole body as brittle as a dried-up leaf. If he was ruthlessly using this proposal to keep her with him for a while after this weekend . . .

"I am."

She took a deep breath, swallowed hard, forced a mocking tone. "After what has gone on between us today?"

"What does that matter?"

"I thought it mattered a great deal."

"It doesn't matter one damn."

"I think it does."

His hands squeezed hers, not enough to hurt her but firmly enough to concentrate her whole being on the intensity of emotion in his eyes. "We're still together, aren't we? You and me, Lissa. Always."

"I. . . I don't know what to say," she murmured. Her heart had stopped beating.

"Don't think," he commanded. "Say, 'Yes, Kane, I will.'"

It wasn't that easy. Lissa found it difficult to take in. It suddenly occurred to her that this was why he had come home this weekend. Why it was so important. Why it was different. Why he had done all the unexpected things he had done, said all he had said. Why he had been so tense, so angry and frustrated and disturbed by her behaviour.

Everything had been leading up to a proposal of marriage. He had decided. And then she had messed his decision around by not giving him the responses he was accustomed to. From her.

*Marriage!*

The shock of it lingered in her mind, making rational thought impossible.

Her heart said yes.

Her head said... wait! Her heart had led her into a lot of loneliness and pain with Kane Marriott.

Her heart pleaded that he was changing, making concessions, looking after her. It cried out for her to toss caution aside, leap into the unknown, be brave, take the chance of having all she wanted with this man.

Her head said they needed more time together before making such a lifetime commitment. More time to be sure it was right.

From her inner turmoil one commonsense question emerged. "Why?" she asked.

Kane never did anything without a reason. There was always a reason. So what reason did he see in marrying her? He had kept her tied to him for a year without having to marry her. Why should he suddenly decide on marriage *now? This* weekend! Or why had he decided before this weekend?

"I want you as my wife," he answered without hesitation. "I want to have children with you. I want you beside me for the rest of our lives."

As plain and as simple as that.

Selection made.

Proving time satisfactory.

Decision taken.

*I have a vision of what I want.* Those were the words Kane had spoken in the car when she had asked if he had a plan for this weekend. She had thought they referred to his business. But this was what had been in his mind. Not his business. Marriage to her!

With a weird sense of unreality, Lissa wondered if he had already set the date for the implementation of his decision.

"I guess you have some idea when this marriage would take place?" she asked.

"A week or so," he stated matter-of-factly.

No frills, of course. A registry office. And no consultation with her about what she might want in the way of a wedding or anything else!

"No," she said.

He seemed to be taken aback. The pressure on her hands tightened a bit more. "What do you mean by that?"

"I mean that if I decide to marry you—and that's by no means certain—it certainly isn't going to take place in a week," she said determinedly.

"Give me one good reason it shouldn't."

All Lissa's bottled-up resentments about Kane's treatment of her came seething to the fore again. "Because I say so," she said grimly.

"That's not a reason," he argued, equally grimly.

"Excuse me, sir..."

Their waiter had arrived to serve their first courses. Lissa had ordered green noodles with crabmeat sauce. He placed the steaming dish in front of her, then mixed the caviar through Kane's prawns Gamberi before serving him. This process gave Lissa time enough to collect herself and remember that Kane probably didn't mean to give offence. He thought his way was eminently reasonable.

The waiter departed.

Kane had forced himself to relax in the interim. He spoke in a calm, controlled tone. "What objection do you have, Lissa?"

Her violet eyes flashed a very purple warning. "If we get married, Kane, I set the date, and I arrange the wedding."

His face slowly softened into a rueful expression. "I thought you'd be like me. Want it as soon as possible."

"I don't." Lissa couldn't imagine any woman not wanting a proper wedding day with all the frills she had ever dreamed of. She was not going to let Kane cheat her out of that because it was not *his* style. He had to start recognising that there were differences between men and women, apart from the differences that *he* found satisfying.

"I guess I am impetuous today."

"You definitely are," Lissa said with feeling. He had her so emotionally confused she had lost her appetite again.

"I'm sorry."

Lissa's eyes widened in surprise. Another apology from Kane? Her heart turned over. He really was changing. For her. She had never known him to apologise for anything before today.

"I'm sorry, too," she said huskily.

"Why?"

"That you didn't understand me better," she explained, privately acknowledging that it was probably as much her fault as his. She should have stood up for herself more all these months, instead of weakly allowing Kane to run things his way.

He shook his head a few times, weighing, pondering her words. "Does that mean you're saying yes to marriage?" he asked.

"I'm thinking about it."

Kane's different manner towards her gave her much food for thought. She picked up her fork and dug into the pasta. Her stomach, she found, was unexpectedly receptive, and her mouth thoroughly enjoyed the taste of the delicate crabmeat sauce. Now that she had recovered from her initial shock, her heart was beating smugly over Kane's concessions. But her mind was very busy.

Maybe it was simply that Kane was skilled at adjusting to a manoeuvring position when he met with a confrontation he was intent on winning. Maybe he didn't care so much what she felt as he cared about getting what he wanted. By hook or by crook. Ruthless, she reminded herself. But honest in his way. She shouldn't forget that. And her heart fluttered exultantly over the thought that Kane wanted her with him for the rest of their lives.

He made considerable inroads into the prawns Gamberi, then asked, "What's there to think about, Lissa?"

"A lot," she replied, and flashed him a sharp look. "Like what the rest of my life is going to be like with you."

"It will be whatever we make of it," he answered reasonably. "Everything always is. What we ourselves make of it. Which is up to us."

"It takes commitment from both people," she pointed out.

"The fact that I've asked you is my commitment."

She couldn't argue with that. It was an irrefutable truth. Once Kane made a decision, that was that. He did stick by what he decided. The big question was, how much giving was he prepared to do in order to make their marriage work? What satisfied him didn't necessarily satisfy her. It certainly hadn't in the past. She had already discovered that loving him was not a recipe for happiness.

"You haven't met my family," she said, unable to keep a touch of resentment out of her voice.

"I'm not marrying them," he said curtly. "I'm marrying you. Let's not muddy the issue."

"I won't be cut off from my family, Kane," she insisted flatly. "Because you don't care for yours, I won't have you saying I shouldn't care for mine. I do. And if you want to marry me, you have to accept that they're part of my life, and they're going to become part of your life, too."

He frowned, not having thought that idea through at all. "If you need them that much..." he temporised.

"Do you want *your* children to cut themselves off from us when they marry?" she pleaded.

His frown deepened. He certainly hadn't thought that far ahead. His mouth twisted into a grimace. "No, I wouldn't want that to happen," he said gruffly.

"My family is important to me," Lissa stated unequivocally.

"All right," he conceded. "I'll meet your parents when it's convenient. This weekend, if you like. If they want to meet me. But they have to accept me, too, Lissa. As I am," he added determinedly.

He was clearly suspicious of families and didn't trust their attitudes. Lissa once again wished she knew more details about his upbringing, but she knew introducing that subject would be fruitless.

"My parents would never interfere with whatever I chose to do, Kane," she said quietly. "No matter what they thought of you, if I chose you as my husband, you would be accepted into the family and made welcome."

His eyes hardened. "*If*, Lissa?"

She met his gaze unwaveringly and stuck to her guns. "I haven't said yes yet, Kane."

"Then why not try saying it?"

Lissa's heart fluttered a nervous protest at pushing too far if the concessions had come to an end. Her mind stubbornly insisted on common sense. "There's too much unresolved between us. And I'd rather work that through before we're married, not after."

Kane's face tightened. A fierce black pride glittered into his eyes. "No. You don't put me on trial, Lissa. I will not be dangled. I'm either the man for you or I'm not.''

''I'll think about it,'' she promised, recklessly pushing to the limit.

She reached it.

Passion flared in his eyes. Determination carved his face into ungiving, relentless lines. ''You don't have to think about it. You either do want to marry me or you don't. If you have to think about it, you don't.''

''That's being totally unreasonable,'' she expostulated.

He didn't budge a millimetre. ''Make up your mind, Lissa. Now!''

Ruthless, decisive Kane. Yet in a way he was right. All the thinking in the world wouldn't change anything. If she didn't marry him, she would regret it all her life. If she did marry him, she would undoubtedly regret that all her life, as well. A bleak prospect. Whatever she did would be wrong.

This *was* the last weekend, she realised. The very last. There was to be no continuation of the kind of relationship they had shared before. Not that she wanted that. Which was why she had decided this was the last weekend. But not in her wildest dreams had she foreseen this development from Kane.

She lifted uncertain eyes to his, reached across the table and took his hands. Her throat tightened but she pushed out the words that would make the decision for her. ''Do you love me, Kane?'' she whispered huskily.

His fingers stroked hers, dragging at the fine skin covering her delicate bones. Maybe she imagined it, but there seemed to be a flicker of vulnerability in his eyes. "Lissa, I can give you more of myself than I ever could, or ever would, to any other person," he said softly. "Does that answer your question?"

It didn't, really. But it answered some questions. It left a lot more up in the air. "Yes," she heard herself saying. I'm weak, she thought. She must be the greatest fool in the world to let herself be satisfied with the limited offer Kane was making. Yet he was right. If you had to think about it, then don't do it. Her heart was having the final say. She was his, and always would be, no matter what the future held.

"You're saying yes to marrying me?" Kane wanted it spelled out. Punctuated. Finalised.

"Yes."

There! It was said! For a moment her words to him on the telephone this morning billowed across her mind, mocking the decision she had just made. What have I done? she thought. What have I done?

She had exchanged the black void for a grey cloud that might have a silver lining, that was what she'd done. And as that answer slid into Lissa's mind, hope banished despair and soothed the torment of doubts.

Kane relaxed into his chair, a small smile curving his lips. The tension, frustration and weariness seemed to wash away from him. He looked refreshed, invigorated. An aura of immense satisfaction seemed to glow around him.

"As soon as possible," he said softly.

Why not, she thought. The die was cast now, for better or for worse. "Six weeks would be the minimum," she said.

"Six weeks it is, then." His smile went crooked. "Does that mean I have to suffer all the buttons and bows in order to tie the knot with you?"

"Frills, too," she insisted.

"You drive a hard bargain, Lissa Gilmore."

"So do you, Kane Marriott."

"Well matched, would you say?"

She sighed. "I have a feeling we're always going to fight over where the line is drawn."

"Oh, I'm sure we'll find some areas of mutual accord," he drawled, and the look in his eyes promised that their marriage bed would certainly be one area where any fighting would be very short-lived.

It teased a smile from her. Kane might not know what love was, but when it came to lovemaking, there was nothing that he didn't know.

He signalled their waiter, who immediately made his way to their table. "A bottle of Veuve Cliquot," Kane requested. "Immediately."

"Yes, sir. Right away," the waiter replied, deftly removing their plates.

She would probably never want for the luxuries of life, Lissa thought, but she didn't think that would mean much if she wasn't happy with Kane. This had to work, she told herself. As Kane said, it was up to them to make it work. Few marriages were made in heaven. They were made with both partners pulling together.

The champagne was brought and poured for them. Kane lifted his glass in a toast. "To us," he said simply.

Lissa clinked her glass to his. "It's up to us," she reminded him.

She remembered Kane's claim that he was a specialist at survival. She was sure now. He would not let their marriage sink if he could save it. That thought made Lissa feel more confident about their future.

"Agreed," he said. "It's up to us."

She looked at Kane, loving the man beyond all reason, and thought that if their marriage did sink... Well, there was no-one she would rather sink with.

Which just went to show she was probably as big a fool as she thought she was. Perhaps that was what last weekends did to people. Instead of doing the sensible thing and breaking up, they got married.

Her eyes sought Kane's in a kind of hopeless hope. "Will we both survive this decision?" she asked whimsically.

A grim irony settled on his face. "I doubt it," he said, "but you know as well as I do... We've got to try."

# CHAPTER SEVEN

ON SUNDAY NIGHT, Lissa drove Kane to the airport for his flight to Melbourne. He didn't meet her parents that weekend. Best to prepare them first, Lissa decided, rather than spring everything on them at once.

Her mind was still whirling with a sense of disbelief and unreality. At the beginning of the weekend she had thought only of breaking her connection to Kane Marriott. At the end of the weekend she was committed to him for life.

Lissa wondered if all women went through such a range of emotions when they became engaged. Perhaps they did. Every woman had to know, as she did, that her life would never be the same again.

Kane kissed her goodbye with the same hungry fervour with which he had greeted her two nights ago, as though he wanted to absorb every part of her, as well as needing to stamp himself on her. "From now on you don't look at another man," he said with a dry little smile. But his eyes were darkly serious.

"I don't want to, Kane," she assured him huskily. "You have my promise that there's only you."

His smile reached his eyes, bathing her in a warm caress. Lissa vowed she would never give him cause to doubt her constancy again. Her vague suggestions of last Friday still niggled him. It seemed strange to Lissa that a man as sure of himself as Kane was had not completely dismissed the issue by now, but she guessed he simply didn't feel sure of other people. Not even her.

The thought depressed her a little as she drove home to the apartment she shared with her brother. Kane had said he could give more of himself to her than he could to anyone else, but she was painfully aware that he withheld total trust. Maybe that was part of being a survivor. What she had to do was convince Kane that she would always stand beside him, no matter what.

Her apartment was one of a big block of apartments at Bondi Junction, and nothing like Kane's. As she walked into it that night, she looked around and reflected that it was an interior decorator's nightmare. She and Tony had collected odd pieces of furniture and added what they fancied to it at various times. There was no style or theme to the decor. However, it was homely and comfortable.

When Tony was there, the place was invariably a mess, but it was tidy right now. Lissa had the apartment to herself for another ten days, until her brother returned from London via Cairo and Singapore. She wished he were here. She wanted to share what she felt with someone. She felt oddly detached from everything, as though she was between two worlds. It was a lonely feeling.

Kane telephoned from Melbourne to wish her good-night. That helped. It made Lissa feel much better. Less lonely. Kane was thinking of her. He was trying.

The only difference of opinion between them during the last two days had been over the engagement ring. With Kane's usual decisiveness, it had been ordered on Saturday morning. Lissa demurred. If he was running so close to the financial wind, as he said, she didn't want him spending a small fortune on her.

Kane had had his own way. "There are some transactions in life, Lissa," he had said somewhat caustically, "where money is not a consideration." And that was that! He chose a beautiful royal blue sapphire surrounded by diamonds, and Lissa closed her ears to the cost of it. It was better if she didn't know.

The ring size had to be altered, and it had been arranged that she pick it up from Prouds on Tuesday. Lissa felt oddly wary of telling anyone the news of her forthcoming marriage until Kane's ring was on her finger. She kept thinking that if something out of the ordinary occurred she could still change her mind. And so could Kane.

Nothing out of the ordinary occurred. Kane didn't change his mind. Neither did she.

On Tuesday afternoon, she accepted the ring from the manager of Prouds, slid it onto the third finger of her left hand and felt fully and officially engaged. Kane telephoned her that night to check that she had it. Somehow that sealed the commitment.

"Have you spoken to your parents yet?" he asked.

"I was about to do it," she said, not wanting him to think she'd had any doubts at all.

"If you change the wedding date to seven weeks, Lissa, I'll be able to afford the time to take you on a real honeymoon. Would you like that?"

A rush of emotional tears blurred her eyes. Kane really was trying to please her, and she felt horribly guilty that she wasn't doing more. "Yes. I'd like that very much," she answered. "Thank you. I'll tell Mum and Dad. Countdown is seven weeks."

She did. Their reactions were fairly predictable— surprise, delight, eagerness to meet the man she was pledged to marry. It was arranged that she and Kane come to lunch next Sunday.

The reaction she had not considered, and which was totally unexpected, was the one she got from Jack Conway. He did not look pleased. In fact, he looked thoroughly miffed. Lissa wondered if he thought he was about to lose her and was vexed over the inconvenience of having to find a replacement, but she soon discovered that was not his concern at all.

"You realise that you're compromised, don't you, Lissa?" he shot at her, the steel-grey eyes unwaveringly fixed on her face.

Lissa stared back uncomprehendingly. "I'm sorry. I don't understand."

"As my secretary you have access, and will have further access, to the information on the Wingicamble and Jessamine projects. Information on what is going to happen there would put Kane Marriott in a position that gives him an overwhelming advantage over his competitors.''

''He would never ask for it.'' She defended Kane hotly. After all, he had had every opportunity over the weekend to press her for what had happened at Friday's board meeting, and he hadn't. ''If he did ask, I wouldn't give it to him,'' she added even more hotly.

Suspicion was withdrawn, but there was a hard, weighing look in Jack Conway's eyes. ''Perhaps not. But I think we'll slot you in somewhere else.''

The managing director of ICAC was not about to take risks with his reputation. No matter how useful Lissa had been to him in the past, she was only a secretary.

Lissa felt that her integrity was impugned. ''I don't want to lose my job, sir,'' she stated, her violet eyes flashing with pride.

''Conflict of interest, my dear.''

''There won't be any conflict,'' Lissa insisted. She didn't want a change of job. She liked being where she was, what she did, the responsibilities her job entailed.

Jack Conway looked dubious. ''I'd hate to think you became a liability instead of an asset, Lissa.''

''It won't happen,'' she said stubbornly.

He regarded her flushed face for several moments, then said, ''I'll think about it.'' But the situation obviously perturbed him.

Which perturbed Lissa.

For the first time she wondered if Kane Marriott would actually consider marrying her in order to get information he thought vitally important to his business. She dismissed the idea. Kane was extreme, but he wasn't that extreme.

When Kane telephoned her that night, Lissa scotched the idea completely. There were far more important things to think about. Like Kane meeting her parents. And arranging a wedding.

The visit with her parents started off well enough. They were impressed with Kane. Handsome, successful, apparently wealthy—Lissa had done well for herself. It was written on their faces. And although Lissa was aware of the inner reserve Kane maintained, he projected an outward charm that made conversation easy.

It was when they came to the wedding plans that things got sticky. Kane obligingly agreed to anything Lissa and her family wanted. The difficulty was that there was no-one that he personally wished to invite. As far as he was concerned, his marriage to Lissa was a private affair. It involved only her and himself.

"Not even any member of your family?" Lissa's mother had protested.

A flat no from Kane. It was a very flat no.

Lissa glossed over the awkward little shock of silence as quickly as she could, but she felt angry with Kane for not making any concessions at all on this point. He was letting her have her way about the wedding ceremony, but he was having his own way, as well. He wanted her married to him. He accepted what she insisted upon but that was it. One look at the stony expression on his face was enough warning to Lissa that this was one of Kane's "take it or leave it" decisions. No room for argument.

Her mother cornered her afterwards, pushing the point that surely a wedding was the best time to effect a family reconciliation. It was a wicked shame that such an estrangement had taken place. Although she did understand that a divorce could make children unforgiving, couldn't Lissa talk Kane around? Surely his parents wouldn't want the rift to go on. And what about his sister? Hadn't Lissa said Kane had a sister?

"I'll talk to him about it, Mum," she had said.

She doubted she would have any success. Kane had laid down the law. Her family had to accept him as he was. All the same, Lissa did think Kane's sister might like to come to his wedding. He visited her occasionally. Wouldn't she be offended if she wasn't asked?

As they drove to the city from Berowra Waters, Lissa decided to broach the subject. After all, the invitations had to be posted this week. Everything had to be settled.

"Kane, your sister..." she started hesitantly.

"No, Lissa!" Curt and to the point.

She bit her tongue.

Kane heaved a sigh and sent her a wry look. "Your parents are nice people. I understand why you want your family to be there. To see you married. To have an ongoing relationship with them. That simply isn't possible with mine, believe me."

"Because you won't let it be possible?" she asked resentfully.

He gave a harsh laugh. "It's not one-sided, Lissa. They hate me as much as I hate them."

"Why?"

His face hardened into grim lines. "Because I made them pay for what they did," he said in a tone that sent a shiver down Lissa's spine.

Something was very wrong.

This wasn't primarily about the trauma of a divorce or an unloved childhood. Lissa tried to recollect everything Kane had ever said about his family. It amounted to very little. She knew that his father had been quite a prominent forensic psychologist who had given expert opinion in criminal trials. Always for the defence.

"He would excuse anything," was one of the very few comments Kane had made about him. The searing contempt in the black eyes had made his opinion clear. There were some things that Kane Marriott would never excuse. Nor forgive. Not ever.

And he obviously hadn't.

Lissa knew nothing about his mother except that she had remarried after the divorce. Kane's sister, she had gathered, was a hopeless neurotic whose husband acted like her nursemaid. That was the sum total of Lissa's knowledge. She now wondered how the daughter of a psychologist had come to be the kind of helpless mess Kane had described.

"I think you'd better explain what they did. And what you did, Kane," Lissa said quietly.

"Leave it," came the curt reply. "It's history."

"No. I've accepted you fobbing me off about your family for a year, Kane. I accepted it because I had no right to know. But I do have a right to understand the man I'm marrying."

He looked at her out of the corner of his eye. "Don't you understand the man you're going to marry?"

"Not always."

His mouth curled. "Neither do I," he said self-mockingly.

"Don't you think you should tell me what happened?" Lissa persisted, quietly determined not to be fobbed off this time.

He shrugged. "It's not a pretty story."

"I don't need pretty stories. I need the truth. If you keep shutting me out of your life, what kind of marriage are we going to have?" she argued.

"One that makes the most of the future," he retorted decisively.

"It's the past that's made you what you are, Kane. Sometimes you say or do things I don't understand. I want to understand. It's time you gave me that understanding."

He frowned. "You won't like it."

"That hardly matters."

There were several moments of tense, considering silence. "True," he finally conceded, then gave her an approving little smile. "That's one thing I like about you, Lissa. You don't flinch from facing the truth."

Yes, she did, Lissa thought. At least, inside she did. But she had given up hiding her head in the sand last weekend. Nevertheless, it was comforting to know that Kane liked her character as well as her femininity.

"So what happened?" she pressed, sternly reminding herself not to flinch, no matter what was revealed.

He relaxed, settling back in the moulded leather seat of the Jaguar. The grimness left his face. His expression was perfectly serene when he began to speak. His voice was dispassionate, devoid of emotion, as if he were merely enunciating a lot of boring, unrelated objects.

"Firstly, I destroyed my father's professional reputation. His supposed integrity."

A frisson of shock ran through Lissa. She hadn't anticipated anything like that! "How?" she asked. She couldn't hold the word back.

"I told the truth."

"My God, Kane!" What kind of man was she marrying? Going to marry? She knew Kane to be hard, but so ruthless?

His gaze did not waver from the road ahead. It was as though he didn't hear her exclamation. There was a quiet, relentless air about him as he went on.

"Then I destroyed my stepfather. Financially. It took a long time," he added grimly, "but I did it."

Lissa sat numbly. What had caused such hatred? There had to be a cause. Kane never did anything without a reason, she told herself.

"I left my mother as close to penury as I could. To live without all the sensuous luxuries that meant far more to her than anything or anyone else," he finished softly.

That's what he had done to his father and stepfather, Lissa quickly realised, taken away what meant most to them. Reputation. Wealth. Pride. Ego.

"Revenge?" she probed, doing her best to keep her voice and the rest of her as calm and dispassionate as he was about all this.

"No. Not revenge. Justice." There was passion in that last word. Harsh passion.

"There's not much mercy there, Kane," Lissa commented softly.

"None," he agreed. "They showed none. They got none. When I was forced to read the Bible at the boarding school where I was sent—to get me out of the way—I learnt more from the Old Testament than I learnt from the new."

"What did they do?"

His mouth curled. His voice took on a light, mocking lilt. "Apart from the wild, drunken, drug-laden orgies? Apart from their obscene obsession with every kind of sexual gratification?"

His jaw clenched. Then slowly unclenched as he forced himself to relax again.

"Apart from that—what happened?" Lissa prompted quietly.

"They corrupted my sister."

It was a flat, unemotional statement of fact. So chilling that Lissa's blood ran cold at the thought of all that was left unsaid. Kane couldn't mean what she thought he meant, could he?

"She . . . joined in?" she asked tentatively.

"No. Not willingly. Jenna was like a mesmerised little rabbit. Helpless. Easily victimised. Conditioned over the years to be that way."

"But not you, Kane."

"No. They couldn't condition me."

Except with hatred and defiance and the will to survive anything, to beat the odds and come out on top, Lissa thought. But his sister . . . Lissa's mind still shied from accepting the kind of truth that Kane's words suggested. Surely she was imagining worse than the actual reality.

"What happened to Jenna?" she blurted, wanting Kane to mitigate the dreadful images he had conjured up.

She saw his mouth thin. "My animal stepfather had his way with her every day she lived with them," he replied with bitter venom. "He had my mother at night as an alternative. My father, who made a profession of excusing any obscenity, refused to believe us, refused to interfere and take Jenna away. My mother did not want to rock the luxury liner she had passage on, so she turned a blind eye to what was happening. She *knew*. And didn't care."

Lissa closed her eyes as a wave of revulsion swept through her. These were the dark memories she had wanted Kane to share with her, the memories that had cured him of strictly carnal desires a long time ago. Oh, she'd read about such things in newspapers, heard about them on television, but Lissa had never expected such horrors to touch her life.

No wonder Kane had kept them to himself! She wished she hadn't asked him. She wished... No, it was better that she knew, no matter how hideous the revelation was. At least it was some help in understanding Kane.

Lissa tried to imagine how it must have been for him, helpless to stop it from happening, helpless to fix it for his sister, a boy of twelve or thirteen pitted against adults determined on holding the status quo. Her heart twisted in sympathy for the boy he had never been allowed to be.

"How did you ruin your stepfather financially?" she asked.

His eyes flashed her a look of black satisfaction. "He owned an engineering company. I set myself up as his rival in business. I hired his best men away from him. That part was easy. He was as much a bastard to work for as he was in all other areas of his life. Then I underbid him on every tender he went for. In short, I stole his business from him. He did a few stupid things in frustration and bankrupted himself. He died of a heart attack soon afterwards. I didn't grieve for him."

Hard, relentless Kane. "You set yourself to do that from when you were still at school?"

"Yes."

This was why his business meant so much to him! Not only was it the means to his own personal success in the world, but every success he had with it undoubtedly fed the satisfaction it had served to give him over the man and woman who had so cruelly and callously victimised his sister.

His hand thumped the steering wheel lightly several times. "Justice," he said, and Lissa imagined his hand was the gavel of a judge on the law bench. "There had to be justice," he affirmed.

Beneath the quiet exterior, Lissa could feel the deep churning emotions. Not all the justice possible could ever undo what had been done, she thought. It punished the guilty, but it didn't save the victims.

"Why didn't Jenna leave?" she asked, sick at heart for the girl who had been robbed of being a girl.

"She was too weak. Too reliant. Too dependent...."

"But she did leave eventually?" Lissa pleaded, wanting there to be some saving grace in this ghastly story.

"Yes. I took her away when I was old enough to control any comeback from them," Kane said flatly. His fingers tightened around the steering wheel, knuckles whitening. "She was a complete mess. A mess for the rest of her life."

He heaved a sigh as though he had to relieve some of the pent-up feelings he had kept rigidly controlled. "I do what I can. I send her a cheque every month so she has some independent means. She knows she can call on me if she needs something. But we are beyond talking to each other. Too much has happened."

So much pain, so many burdens to carry in the dark recesses of his mind and heart and soul. No wonder he didn't trust anyone! No wonder he was a loner! Lissa thought of her own relatively easy, trouble-free life and marvelled that he had been strong enough to become the man he was.

Lissa had no sympathy for his father or mother or stepfather. She couldn't excuse or forgive that kind of wickedness.

Kane would never ask if she approved or disapproved of what he had done. Proud. Resolute. A law unto himself. But he was her man, and if doing what he had done had helped him to resolve any of the pain they had inflicted, she was not about to criticise his actions. She was on his side.

"I'm sorry, Kane," she said sadly.

He flashed her a wary look that had more than a hint of raw vulnerability. Lissa knew intuitively he had never revealed what he had told her to anyone else and she met his stabbing look unflinchingly, aware he needed to know that her sympathy was sincere. It was an important moment, a matter of trust extended to her, returned to him.

"Thank you for telling me," she added, instinctively reaching across to touch him. Her long, delicate fingers curled over his thigh, pressing lightly and lovingly.

His gaze flicked to the road but he dropped a hand from the steering wheel to cover hers and hold it there. "I want my memories of our wedding to be happy, Lissa," he said gruffly.

"They will be," she assured him.

"That's why none of my family will be there."

A man alone.

Except for her.

Lissa's heart went out to him.

"Could you catch a later flight tonight?" she asked huskily.

"I guess so. Why?" He shot her a wry look. "More of your family for me to meet?"

She returned an inviting smile. "No. I thought we might go to your apartment and make love."

Uncertainty flitted over his face, as though he couldn't quite believe she could put his past history aside so readily.

"You need me, don't you?" she asked, wanting that reassurance from him.

"Yes." Fervent. Unequivocal.

"We'll be happy together?"

The dark eyes flashed determination. "Yes."

Lissa relaxed, feeling a warm rush of hope that Kane would come to love her as she wanted him to. At last he was beginning to share his life with her, the bad with the good. "Let's make love twice."

His face relaxed into a smile. "Nymphomaniac."

"If you don't think you can..." she teased.

Another flash of his eyes. Hot simmering chocolate. He would. He could hardly wait to prove he could. With immense pleasure.

Much later, they lay entwined in the languorous aftermath of blissful satisfaction. "I want a family, Lissa," Kane confided. "A family of my own that will be how a family should be. I want to give my kids a good upbringing. Be the kind of father I wished I'd had. You want a family, too, don't you?"

"Yes, of course," she murmured happily. It was not an immediate ambition, but Lissa had always assumed that would be an integral part of her life somewhere along the line. To her it belonged to the natural cycle of life.

Kane's chest rose and fell beneath her in a sigh of contentment. "We'll make good parents."

She smiled, curling the hair below his throat around her finger. "We can but try. But I guess we'll make our share of mistakes, Kane. Nobody's perfect."

"Your parents did a fine job with you."

More approval. She was learning a lot about how Kane thought of her today. All of it good. "Thank you," she said, and kissed the pulse at the base of his throat.

His fingers threaded through the thick waves of her hair and held her head there. "You'll have to show me how to do it," he said, his voice a low throb, matching his pulse.

"Do what?" She kissed him again.

"Be a good parent."

Her laugh was a gurgle of delight in his confidence in her. "I haven't had any more practice than you have, Kane."

"But you've had a good example. That has to help."

She sighed in contentment. "I'm glad you were impressed by my parents."

"There's no harm in them."

Lissa wondered if that was the rule by which Kane judged people. It wouldn't surprise her if it was, given his experience. She felt much closer to him than she had ever felt before, beginning to understand the mind that drove the man.

He had to succeed. His obsessiveness about that was based on an insecurity Lissa had never known. It was only natural his business had top priority. To him it was something tangible, reachable, concrete. Results could be counted, profits banked. People were much less predictable.

Kane might not know what love was, but he had chosen her above all the other women he could have drawn to him, and today he had begun to trust her, to confide in her. He wanted *her* as his wife, *her* to give him the family he dreamed of having. That meant something. It meant a lot to Lissa.

Kane Marriott was a hard, uncompromising man, but she could rely on loyalty and fidelity and his absolute commitment to their marriage. Apart from which, he was willing to learn, if she could find the right way to teach him. There were no guarantees in life, Lissa told herself. All they could do was try to make the best of what they had together.

## CHAPTER EIGHT

IT WAS A SMALL WEDDING, but with all the frills that Lissa had ever envisaged. Her mother declared it the most lopsided wedding in history, with only the groom on his side, but Lissa steadfastly supported Kane's insistence on standing alone. He wanted her beside him. Only her. For the rest of his life. That was the whole point of getting married.

Nevertheless, as she walked down the aisle on her father's arm, Lissa had a sinking feeling in her stomach. Had Kane's feelings for other people been completely anaesthetised by his family? What if he could never give her the love she wanted from him? What if she ever let him down, by the standards he expected of her? Would he judge her with his chilling black and white ruthlessness? No grey? To marry Kane Marriott was a wildly dangerous thing to do.... So why was she doing it?

Because there is no reasonable alternative, her heart insisted.

Her mind told her the problems would come later.

Her heart was hammering out the "Last Post" as her father handed her over to the man who was waiting to claim her as his wife. Kane smiled at her, his eyes warmly saying she looked beautiful and exquisitely feminine in her bridal finery. And he wanted her beside him. Only her. For the rest of his life.

Lissa couldn't deny him.

For better or for worse, she loved Kane Marriott.

So she married him.

From the moment the fateful words were said, Lissa was no longer a nervous bride, but a deliriously happy one. All the guests said so. Her family said so. Lissa knew that how she looked had nothing to do with happiness. She was simply seized by a heady feeling of recklessness. Whatever the consequences, she would face them when they arose. And overcome them. There was no turning back. She had made her bed. There was nothing left to do now but lie in it. With Kane. Together they would face and share whatever came of their lives.

There was a different quality about Kane's lovemaking on their wedding night. Or perhaps it was a different feeling inside Lissa. They had been lovers for a year, knew each other intimately in every physical sense, yet it was as if Kane were touching her for the first time, kissing her for the first time, with a slow, tender caring that she had never known from him before.

It was beautiful and deeply emotional to her, and when he finally joined with her, the bonding seemed so meaningful that tears rushed to her eyes, and she wound her arms and legs around him and hugged him tightly to her, fiercely possessive of this man who was now hers to have and to hold from this day forth.

"I love you, Kane," she whispered, giving up her heart to him. "I do love you."

"Lissa," was all he whispered in reply, but her ears heard love in her name, and her heart was content with the inarticulate response because of the giving implicit in his touch, in his kisses, in the body cleaving to hers.

It *was* different, Lissa realised. She was Kane's wife. The commitment was complete. She was his woman. He was her man. There would never be anyone else on either side.

The honeymoon was meant to be idyllic, and it started that way, except for one small difference of opinion Lissa quickly erased. The morning after the wedding they flew out of Sydney for Fiji. Kane had booked ten days for them on Turtle Island, a small, exclusive resort that catered for a dozen couples at a time. It was there that the two movies of *Blue Lagoon* had been filmed, and from the moment they arrived, Lissa was entranced with the tropical paradise. However, their first night on the island was slightly marred by Kane's dubious reaction to Lissa's using contraceptive precautions.

He thought they had agreed on having a family, which they had, but Lissa hadn't anticipated he meant straight away. Becoming pregnant on their honeymoon didn't seem like a good idea to her. Once they were settled into their marriage, she would be very happy to have a baby, but straight away seemed rather premature to her.

Kane did not argue. He said it was her body and her choice. Nevertheless, some of the ardour seemed to go out of his lovemaking. He was still caring of her pleasure, yet Lissa sensed she had disappointed him, and it made her feel guilty. He had been trying to please her. She wanted to please him.

Besides, she argued to herself, lots of people tried for months—years—to have a baby. It wasn't all that likely that she would get pregnant before she and Kane had had quite a bit of living together—time to sort out the problems that constant proximity might raise, and become comfortable with each other.

Lissa's decision to do away with all precautions was rewarded by the happy glow in Kane's eyes when she told him of it. For the rest of their stay on Turtle Island Lissa had no reason to doubt Kane's ardour. Which made her very happy.

One idyllic day followed another. The weather could not have been better. They rode horses around the island before breakfast. They swam or snorkelled or lay idly reading in their private double hammock under the palm trees until lunchtime. They made love in the heat of the afternoon. They played beach volleyball with the Fijian staff until sunset. They drank cocktails with the other guests and enjoyed the general conversation over dinner. They made love long into the night.

Most of the time Lissa forgot about getting pregnant, but she could not help wondering if Kane thought about it every time he left his seed inside her. He did not mention it. Neither did she. It no longer mattered. They were in accord. Until their honeymoon came to an abrupt end.

It was on the fifth day that the fax came from Melbourne. Another crisis. The men on Kane's construction site had voted to follow their union's recommendation to the whole industry that they strike for higher pay. They had walked off the job.

There was no discussion about what should be done. Kane's business was in jeopardy. There was no other consideration to be taken into account. He immediately made his decision and booked flights to get them to Australia the next day. Then he broke the news to Lissa.

No "I'm sorry the honeymoon is over."

His mind was totally taken up with his financial problems.

Which was reasonable, Lissa told herself. If this strike sent his engineering company to the wall, everything Kane had built out of his life would be shattered. It wasn't as if she hadn't known she took second place to his business. And she knew why it meant so much to him. She truly had no complaint about what he'd done. It was the manner in which he'd done it that hurt. No sharing. Completely unilateral. Kane being Kane, not her husband.

Lissa decided that wasn't good enough. She was his wife, and she wasn't going to let him treat her like a weekend girlfriend he could pick up or put down as it suited him. What happened to his business would affect her, too, so she had every right to be involved.

"I'll go to Melbourne with you," she said.

He frowned at her.

"We do have another week of our honeymoon left before I have to go back to work," she pointed out. "I'm not going to stay in Sydney alone, Kane."

"Lissa, it won't be pleasant for you," he warned. "If I'm going to pull this out of the fire, I'll be working day and night." He frowned again. "You could stay on here if you like. I'm sorry I didn't think of that. If you want...."

"No. I don't want to stay here without you, Kane. I'll explore Melbourne. I've never been there, so I'm sure I'll find lots to see and do. And who knows? You might find some use for me. I'm a good secretary, you know."

The dark eyes probed hers uncertainly. "You won't mind my not being able to dance attendance on you? Not being able to meet you for lunch or dinner? Coming in late and disturbing your sleep?"

She walked over to him, slid her hands around his neck, moved her body provocatively against his and said, "You can disturb my sleep anytime, Kane."

Then she kissed him.

His response lasted well into their last night on Turtle Island. There was no more argument about her accompanying him to Melbourne for the last week of their honeymoon.

However, things didn't work out as Lissa had hoped they would. Throughout her stay in Melbourne she felt lonely and bored. It was no fun exploring a city by herself, and she saw very little of Kane. Some nights she was asleep when he returned to the hotel. He didn't wake her. Even though they made love in the mornings, he was tense and on edge again by the time they sat down to breakfast.

He would rouse himself to ask what her plans were for the day, but he didn't really listen to her reply. His mind was occupied with what he had to do. When she asked about his problems, he would only mutter that they were bad. By the end of the week Lissa was glad enough to fly home to Sydney, even though Kane had to remain in Melbourne. At least she would have her job to occupy her and people she knew around her.

Jack Conway had kept her on as his secretary despite his misgivings about her compromised position. Apparently he had decided to trust her integrity. She was, after all, very useful to him. He seemed pleased to see her on her first morning back.

"How was the honeymoon?" he asked, his steel-grey eyes glinting with interest.

"Great!" Lissa replied. Her pride and her loyalty to Kane prevented any revelation that the second half of it had been rather miserable.

"The strike didn't put a damper on it?" her boss asked shrewdly.

Lissa could have kicked herself. Of course he knew about the strike! It affected ICAC, as well. She forced a smile. "It shortened our holiday. That's all."

"Ah!" One eyebrow lifted in inquiry. "Marriott hasn't asked you about the Wingicamble and Jessamine projects yet?"

Lissa frowned at the question. "No, sir," she answered firmly.

Jack Conway's mouth twisted in ironic appreciation. "Interesting... Must have other irons in the fire.
I wonder..."

He drifted off to his office, leaving Lissa wondering, as well. Jack Conway obviously expected Kane to
use her as a source of information. That he hadn't was
certainly teasing her boss's mind. The managing director of ICAC wouldn't think twice about using her
to his advantage. He had done so over and over again.
Was Kane knowingly using silence through her as a
lever to manipulate the situation? Was he waiting for
her to tell him, expecting her to alleviate the financial
pressure he was feeling?

Lissa dismissed the speculation after a while. It was
all too devious for her. Kane had not asked her for information, and she was satisfied with that. Although
she did wonder how he had brought about his stepfather's financial ruin, and by what means it had been
accomplished. He must have had inside information
to knowingly undercut tenders. How else could he
have done it? But that was different, justified, Lissa
told herself.

Being separated from her husband was not the most
satisfactory start to their marriage, she thought despondently, particularly as one week stretched into
another. Kane telephoned her most mornings before
she went to work, but she grew restive with the situation. She was no longer even a weekend wife. Although the union strike had ended, Kane explained
that there was so much work to make up that he
couldn't possibly leave it. He had offered the men

overtime and they were taking it, but everything had to be properly coordinated and supervised.

The waiting wasn't easy. Despite her fair-minded reasoning, Lissa couldn't help feeling neglected and unimportant. It was depressing being alone night after night. Sometimes she felt like crying out of sheer frustration. She had married the man she loved, but she certainly didn't have him. She didn't have his love, either. She doubted that any man could be less lover-like than Kane Marriott on the telephone.

On the Friday night of the second week, she had a few moments of dizzying hope that Kane had changed his mind about not coming home for the weekend. Lissa knew of no-one else who would call her at ten o'clock at night, so when the telephone rang, she flew to answer it.

"Lissa Marriott," she rattled out, taking pleasure in giving her new married name.

"Who are you?"

A woman's voice! Lissa's heart fell with a dull thump. Suspicion crawled into her mind. Why would any woman be calling Kane at this hour?

"I'm Lissa Marriott, Kane's wife!" she said coldly. "What do you want?"

"I want Kane."

"I'm afraid Kane isn't here at the moment. He's tied up with business in Melbourne."

Silence.

"Would you like to leave a message?" Lissa asked with acid sweetness. "I'll pass it on for you."

More silence.

Well, that put a stop to that, Lissa thought with grim satisfaction.

Then finally a reply, wavering with shock and uncertainty. "Did you say... his... *wife?*"

"Yes," said Lissa with firm emphasis. Her temperature started to rise. If Kane had lied to her... If he hadn't been constant to her from the beginning... "Who's speaking, please?" she demanded tersely.

More silence. Then, "I'm Jenna Woodbury. I'm Kane's sister." Said faintly, as though unsure of her position.

"I'm sorry," Lissa said quickly. "I didn't realise it was you. I didn't know...."

The responding voice still sounded uncertain. Shaky. "He... he didn't tell me he was married." Even more uncertain, worried. "I'm sorry. I'll have to go."

"No! Don't do that!" Lissa protested sharply. She wanted to talk to Jenna. There was so much to find out.

"I don't want to interfere...."

"You're not interfering!" Lissa rushed out, then didn't know what to say. "I am married to your brother," she stressed. She couldn't very well blurt out that Kane hadn't wanted his sister at their wedding. "I'm sorry we haven't met," she frantically improvised. "I did want to...." This was so frightfully embarrassing!

The reply came slowly. "Do you think...?' There was a query in it, an uncertainty that needed resolving.

"Yes, I do," Lissa said firmly, hoping it was the right encouragement.

"I'd...I'd like to meet you." Very hesitant.

To Lissa's ears there was a note of real distress behind the words. She felt an acute wave of sympathy for the victimised little girl Jenna had been, for the neurotic mess of a woman she had become. She suddenly remembered Kane saying that his sister called on him when she needed something. "Jenna, is there anything I can do for you? Kane's away, but I could do whatever you want."

A few more moments of silence, then tentatively, "Would you...? Could you...? I need someone to talk to."

"Of course I'll talk to you."

"Could we have lunch?"

"Yes. Anything you like," Lissa rushed out impulsively, not stopping to think whether Kane would approve or not. "Wherever you like," she affirmed strongly.

"That would be good."

"What about tomorrow? Or when would it suit you, Jenna?"

"Tomorrow. Thank you." A deep breath, then agitatedly, "What's your name?"

"Lissa. It's really Melissa, but everyone calls me Lissa. Where shall we meet for lunch? Do you have a favourite place? Would you like to come here, Jenna?"

"No! Oh, no! Not without Kane being there. I wouldn't impose...." Another deep breath in an attempt to calm the sudden edge of anxiety. "What about Doyle's at Circular Quay? We could watch the boats on the harbour. And Kane needn't know."

It was as if Jenna felt she had to offer a side attraction, and there was definitely some worry about her brother's reaction to their meeting. Right at that moment, Lissa didn't care what Kane thought. The urge to appease his sister for any offence committed against her was paramount in Lissa's mind. Kane might consider Jenna weak and neurotic, but dear heaven! What she had suffered. . . .

"That's fine by me," Lissa agreed fervently. "Twelve o'clock?"

"Yes. Twelve. Thank you, Lissa. Woodbury is my name. Jenna Woodbury. Will you remember that?"

Still that edge of anxiety. "No problem," Lissa assured her. "I'll look forward to meeting you."

"It's . . . it's nice of you to say so. I'm glad Kane found someone he wanted to marry. Very glad. . . ."

Her voice trailed off. Lissa was left floundering again. "Well, I'll see you tomorrow, Jenna."

"Yes. Tomorrow. Good night, Lissa."

It was several minutes after the call had ended before Lissa realised that she hadn't found out why Jenna had called Kane. She mustn't forget to ask tomorrow, she told herself distractedly. If Jenna needed something, Kane would want her to have it.

It had been such a strange conversation, with so many implications running through it. Lissa recoiled from the idea, but it seemed as though Jenna thought

Kane was ashamed of his relationship with her. Surely that wasn't true. And yet . . . Lissa shook her head in confusion. There was so much she didn't know. Perhaps tomorrow's meeting with Jenna would make everything much clearer.

LISSA MADE SURE she was at Circular Quay in good time for her date with Kane's sister. If Jenna was as neurotic as Kane claimed, any little disturbance—like being made to wait a few minutes—might upset her. For some reason, Lissa felt that getting to know Jenna Woodbury was important. In understanding his sister, she might get a better insight into Kane. It was strange, one so strong, the other so weak. Lissa simply didn't know what to expect. On the other hand, Jenna might not keep the date at all. Lissa's main concern was not to be at fault herself.

She had worn the violet dress that Jack Conway had admired. It was one of Lissa's favourites and she hoped Jenna would think she looked nice. Lissa had no idea what Kane's sister looked like. Dark haired, dark eyed, she imagined, but when she entered Doyle's, precisely at noon, and asked for the table booked in the name of Woodbury, she found the reality far different from the image in her mind.

She was led to a table occupied by a couple, not a woman by herself. The man rose at her approach. He looked to be around forty, his brown hair liberally streaked with grey, his face rather nondescript but pleasant enough, average height, average build.

The woman at the table was an exceptionally pretty blonde, her face delicately featured and dominated by large brown doelike eyes, soft, liquid wounded eyes. Impossible to relate her to Kane at all. It happened in families, of course, that brothers and sisters didn't look at all alike. She stared at Lissa, drinking in every detail of her as the man introduced himself and his wife.

"I'm Trevor Woodbury," he said, exuding kindness and caring. "My wife is agoraphobic. People and crowds discomfit Jenna, so I brought her in myself so she would feel safe. I'll leave you to look after her now." His blue eyes appealed anxiously to Lissa to treat his wife with care before turning to his wife. "You know where I'll be, darling. Come and get me when you want to go. Come and get me for any reason, at any time at all."

"You're wonderfully kind, Trevor," she said tremulously.

He squeezed her hand reassuringly, held Lissa's chair for her, saw her comfortably seated, ordered drinks for them and left.

"I hope you like seafood, Lissa," Jenna began nervously.

Doyle's was famous for its fresh seafood. "I love it," she assured Kane's sister, hoping to put her at ease.

They both studied the menu, gave their lunch order to a waiter, then suffered through an awkward impasse, studying each other until Lissa thought of something to say.

"Your husband is a loving, gentle man."

Jenna's smile illuminated her face. She was quite heart-wrenchingly lovely, Lissa thought. Kane had said his sister had been corrupted, but there was not a trace of depravity on her fine face. Nor in her clothes, a modest grey suit and a high-necked, frilly pink blouse.

"Trevor saved me," she said simply.

Which left a gap in the conversation.

"Kane told me what you suffered through," Lissa offered awkwardly.

Jenna leaned forward, her face earnestly wanting Lissa to understand. "If it hadn't been for Trevor I would have taken my own life. He's a male nurse, you know."

"No. I didn't know that." Only that he nursed Jenna, according to Kane.

"I met him at the drug rehabilitation centre. That was the best thing Kane did for me, putting me in there. If I hadn't met him . . . My husband is the most loving man in the world."

Lissa smiled. "I can see that. You're very lucky, Jenna."

"Yes. I am. Kane tried all he could. He always did. But he never understood." Anxiety edged her voice as she quickly added, "Please don't think I'm criticising Kane."

"Not everyone is good at understanding," Lissa soothed.

The big brown eyes looked searchingly at her. "I think you must be very brave." She nodded, as though satisfied with what she saw in Lissa's face. "And strong. Of course, Kane wouldn't marry anyone who wasn't strong. You have to be strong."

Lissa was hopelessly bemused by this off-the-top judgment of her. "Why do you say that?"

Jenna gave a nervous little laugh. "Weakness upsets him. He doesn't know how to deal with it. That's not his fault, you know. It's simply not in his character. Kane is a born fighter."

"Yes. I guess he is," Lissa agreed. The ultimate survivor, she thought, no matter what cost was involved to the walking wounded along the way.

"You love him."

It was a statement, not a question.

"Yes," Lissa answered, unable to deny such directness.

"How long have you known him?"

"A little over a year."

"And when did you marry?"

"Four weeks ago today."

Jenna nodded. Lissa again felt acutely embarrassed that Jenna had not received an invitation to the wedding, that Kane had not seen fit for them to meet before this.

Jenna looked up, saw the telltale flush on her face and smiled sympathetically. "It's all right. I understand. Kane would want to keep this separate from the past. A new, clean life. He has told you, hasn't he?"

What she meant did not have to be spelled out. The knowledge was in both sets of eyes, and the almost childlike directness of Jenna's gaze made evasion seem wrong. "Some of it," Lissa admitted, painfully aware that she might be giving pain.

"Does he love you, Lissa?"

Somehow it seemed impossible not to tell the truth. "I don't know," she replied honestly. "He's beginning to trust me."

Jenna smiled. "I'm glad. He's been alone for so long. Terribly alone. I couldn't help him. Not the way he needed help. I wasn't the right person."

"You love him very much, don't you, Jenna?" Lissa said quietly.

"Oh, yes." Tears blurred her eyes and she hastily blinked them back. "I'd do anything for him. I want him to be happy. It's not been an easy life for him, either. He coped differently from me. I hope you can be patient with him, Lissa. He won't let it show, but he hurts inside. Sometimes I think it was worse for him than it was for me. I know it hurt him to see me. It still hurts him to see me. There's nothing I can do about that. He thinks I let him down," she said sadly.

"I'm sorry," Lissa whispered, her heart going out to the girl who had virtually lost the brother she loved. She thought over all Kane had told her, why it hurt him to see his sister now, then softly asked, "Why didn't you leave the situation, Jenna? Why did you stay with your mother and stepfather?"

Her lips wobbled in a half smile. "Oh, I couldn't leave," she said decisively. "There was no other solution that was viable."

There was a strength of purpose in those tortured brown eyes that hadn't been there before—a spark that burned beyond the ashes of her life. Lissa retreated before that look, confused, trying to understand, realising that Jenna was trying to tell her something that was very simple to her but was frighteningly complex to Lissa.

She tried to hedge around the subject, probing for some kind of insight. "I realise ... it must have been so very difficult for a twelve-year-old—"

"That had nothing to do with it!" Jenna interrupted quickly. "Nothing at all!" The spark was swallowed by a blurring wave of bewilderment. "I thought you'd understand. But you don't."

She started to rise, picking up her bag, confusion and distress in every agitated movement. Lissa impulsively reached across the table and placed her hand over Jenna's to concentrate her attention.

"I'm trying to understand," she said in apologetic appeal. "Please don't go. Please... I want to listen to you. I want you to tell me what I don't understand."

It seemed to work. Jenna settled down again, stopped moving, yet her stillness had a brittle quality. The big brown eyes focused on Lissa's with intense concentration, studying her sincerity. "If I only had to consider myself, I would have left," she said, her voice firm with her own inner logic. "Twelve years old or not. I am not that weak."

"Then ... why?" Even as she asked the question Lissa saw the pained flicker of dismissal in Jenna's eyes and knew she had failed the test of understanding.

"It's simple, really," Jenna muttered, then fidgeted into moving again, pushing back her chair, checking that she had her handbag, standing up. Her eyes evaded Lissa's. "I must go back to Trevor."

"Yes, of course," Lissa stated numbly. She couldn't force this victimised woman to do anything. She had to agree with whatever Jenna wanted. Referring to what had happened all those years ago had emotionally disturbed her. Lissa could have kicked herself for introducing the subject. She should have been more tactful. For a first meeting. . . .

Jenna took a couple of steps, hesitated, looked at Lissa again. "I like you. I'm glad I met you."

"I like you, too," Lissa returned softly.

Jenna nodded.

Their meals arrived. Jenna frowned at the plates as the waiter set them on the table. She gave a little shake of her head and started to move away again, as though the food had nothing to do with her. What a mess I've made of this, Lissa thought grimly.

She snatched up her own handbag, intent on leaving the money to pay for the meal. She felt impelled to see that Jenna reached her husband safely, wherever he was. She dropped the required notes on the table, rose to her feet, turned in time to see Jenna swing on her heel and step towards her.

"Lissa . . ."

"Yes?"

Jenna returned to their table, each step deliberately purposeful, a resolute look on her face. She stopped in front of Lissa. "It happened because . . ."

"Yes?" Lissa encouraged softly.

A shudder ran through Jenna's slight body, but the resolution didn't waver. "I desperately wanted to leave that house. But Kane's solution was for me to run away with him. He said he'd lie about his age and get a job and look after me. He would have done it, too. He was big enough by then. And always so strong. But I couldn't let him give up his chance at a good life. So I had to stay. There was no other way."

The wounded brown eyes flashed with inner strength, the conviction of absolute certainty. The same strength made her voice firm as she gave her reason. No quiver of doubt. Simple, direct, unquestionable.

"I had to protect Kane."

Then suddenly Trevor was there at his wife's side, gently taking her arm. "Want to go now, darling?" he asked, his voice kind, soothing.

Jenna flashed him a relieved smile. "Yes."

He directed an appeal at Lissa. "You'll excuse us?"

"Of course." She reached out and squeezed Jenna's hand. "Thank you for meeting me. And talking to me."

Jenna searched her eyes anxiously. "Kane won't like it. I only wanted to see . . . to know you a little. You won't tell him, will you, Lissa?"

The idea of any deception sat uncomfortably on Lissa, yet she couldn't reject the appeal in the liquid brown eyes. "If you'd rather I didn't. . . ."

Jenna gave her a loving smile, instantly forgiving Lissa's slowness in comprehending what was perfectly obvious to her. "I'm glad Kane found you."

"I'm glad you found your husband, Jenna." She looked at Trevor with deep respect for the depth of his giving. "Thank you."

The blue eyes lost their reserve and bestowed warm approval on her. "Please stay and have your lunch. I'll fix everything at the desk."

He led his wife away.

Lissa sat down at the table again. She picked at the meal in a desultory fashion as she struggled to understand what she had been told. Somehow this went far past sex and sexuality. Had she been listening to the ravings of a very disturbed person? Or had she seen a person who had made the ultimate sacrifice by having paid the price of being the ultimate victim?

Lissa had no appetite. She gave up on the meal and wandered out to the boardwalk that edged the busy waterway of Circular Quay. She sat on one of the many benches, idly watching the activity on the harbour and the pedestrians who strolled by her, people going about their lives, all their private personal secrets hidden from view.

She worried over not telling Kane about this meeting with his sister, yet perhaps Jenna knew her brother better than she did. Kane might fiercely resent her stepping in where she wasn't supposed to tread, particularly since she was sure Jenna was right about his desire for a clean new life.

Whatever the truth of the past, at least Jenna had a new lease on life with Trevor. Perhaps it was better to let sleeping dogs lie. Lissa didn't want to create trouble between brother and sister. What she had to do was concentrate on her marriage to Kane . . . if he started giving it a chance.

She rose despondently from the bench and set off for home. It was only then that she realised she hadn't found out why Jenna had telephoned Kane. Probably something personal between sister and brother, Lissa decided. Nothing to do with her. Yet somehow it was difficult to accept that Jenna had to be rejected from the life she was to share with Kane. It felt wrong.

# CHAPTER NINE

THE TROUBLING QUESTIONS about Kane's family relationships faded abruptly into the background when Lissa began to suspect she was pregnant. The day after meeting Jenna she realised her normal monthly cycle was running very late. Not only that, but her breasts felt tight and overly sensitive. Then on Tuesday and Wednesday mornings she suffered a slight queasiness. The idea that she had conceived a child made her feel panicky.

She wasn't ready to have a baby. It was all very well agreeing to a family in theory, but faced with the reality, Lissa felt intensely apprehensive about the consequences. She didn't really feel she had a marriage, with Kane having been away all the time. Yet maybe having a baby would make all the difference in the world to their relationship.

If it had happened, there was no point in not facing up to it, Lissa decided. She bought a pregnancy-test kit and carried out the test first thing on Thursday morning. Strangely enough, she felt extremely nervous about the result until the test showed positive. Then, despite all her misgivings about her future with Kane, an exhilarating excitement raced through her veins and reduced her mind to sentimental mush.

A baby. Her baby. Kane's baby. Their very own child. Made by them.

She was still in a daze of absurd happiness when Kane made his usual morning telephone call. She raced to answer it, her heart leaping madly at the thought of telling Kane he was going to be a father. Was a father.

"Lissa?" his voice came brusquely.

"Yes," she breathed ecstatically.

"I'm coming home today. I'll probably get to the apartment before you make it back from work, so don't worry if the lights are on. Okay?"

Delight dizzied her. Kane was coming home. Right at the best moment. Not even waiting for the weekend. She didn't want to tell him the news over the telephone. She wanted to see his face when she told him about the baby. What a wonderful night it was going to be!

"Yes. That's marvellous, Kane!" she gushed in wild joy. "Is everything all right now?"

A pause, then, "We'll talk about it tonight, Lissa."

"I can hardly wait," she bubbled. "It seems like forever since we've been together."

"Yes. It does," he agreed.

"Don't let anything change your mind," she pleaded.

"I won't."

She heaved a happy sigh of satisfaction. "I'll try to get home early. I'll cook you the best dinner you've had in weeks."

"Lissa..." There was a slight edge to his voice. She heard him sigh. "I'll look forward to that, Lissa," he said softly. "But don't go to too much trouble."

She laughed. "You mean we won't get around to eating?"

"Probably not," he replied dryly.

Her pulse leapt in anticipation. She had missed him so much. How would he make love to her when he knew about the baby? She melted at the thought.

"Lissa..." Very gravelly.

He wanted her as much as she wanted him, Lissa thought exultantly. "Yes?"

"Never mind," he rasped. "I'll see you tonight. 'Bye now."

Lissa was floating on cloud nine as she went to work that morning. Every time she had to stop her car for a red light, she couldn't resist sliding a hand over her stomach. It was crazy how maternal and protective she felt, while bubbling with happy anticipation at the same time. It was a miracle she made it to the ICAC building without some mishap. Her concentration on driving was shot to pieces.

"You look particularly glowing this morning, Lissa," was Jack Conway's dry comment when he looked her over.

"Thank you, sir," she replied with a secretive little smile. She couldn't tell him why. Not before she told Kane.

"Marriage must be agreeing with you," her boss observed, his mouth curving into what could almost be a benevolent smile. "You're a good girl, Lissa."

Such an unexpected compliment, along with the uncharacteristic manner from Jack Conway, left Lissa momentarily speechless.

"One thing about Marriott.... He always delivers what he promises," her boss continued. "Sticky situation he had in Melbourne, but he's pulling it through. We've decided on giving him the Wingicamble and Jessamine projects. The public announcement won't be made for another month, but I'll give him a call tomorrow. Have a quiet word with him. I want him geared up for our jobs. Stop him from going after other projects. Not to our best advantage if he's overextended."

"I'm sure Kane would appreciate that, Mr. Conway," Lissa said eagerly, her inner happiness bursting into a dazzling smile. She knew how much those projects meant to Kane, and such good business news coming on top of the news of the baby would surely make him very happy.

Jack Conway's steel-grey eyes actually twinkled. "The man has impeccable judgment. Like me. After all, we both picked you," he joked, then went off chuckling.

Lissa heaved a rueful sigh. Despite Jack Conway's pride or pleasure in her, she was quite sure that pregnancy did not project the kind of class image the managing director of ICAC wanted in his secretary. It would undoubtedly mean the end of her job here.

Kane would probably insist she stop working any-how. He wouldn't want any risk taken with *his* child.

What she would do with herself until the baby was born, Lissa had no idea. She told herself she would think of something. Although it would be strange not having a job to go to. On the other hand, she now had other, more important responsibilities.

The lights were on in the apartment when she got home. Kane didn't come rushing outside to meet her. Probably taking a shower, Lissa thought. She hurried through the conservatory to the kitchen. The shopping bags of fresh food she had bought for their possible dinner were hastily dumped on the counter. She was heading through the dining room to the staircase when she saw Kane rise from one of the leather sofas in the living room.

"You're here!" she said in surprise, her feet instantly coming to a halt, her heart bolting with pleasure and excitement.

"Yes. I'm here," he repeated with sardonic weariness.

No light of pleasure in his eyes at seeing her. He looked burnt out, haggard, the skin on his face stretched tightly over the bones. He held a glass of whiskey in his hands, and there was something in the loose-limbed way he moved that made Lissa think it was not the first drink he'd had today.

Her excitement fizzled. Something was wrong. Badly wrong. She watched him come towards her, sensed the explosive coil of tension inside him despite the relaxed stroll of his approach.

"Hard day?" he asked.

"No," she answered, but she knew he wasn't listening. He had mouthed those words to cover his thoughts. There was a blind, fixed look in the black eyes.

"I'll get you a drink," he said, and walked right past her.

He hadn't even stopped to kiss her! Lissa stared after him in pained incredulity. What kind of greeting was that from a man who had been away from his wife for three weeks? A frightened agitation played havoc with Lissa's nerves as she followed him as far as the doorway into the kitchen.

Kane had to be in deep trouble. His first instinct in times of extreme danger would be to isolate himself. He wanted no-one near him. If he was going down, his pride would insist that he go alone.

She watched him drop a couple of ice-cubes into a glass and felt a chill run around her blood. There was no true sharing with Kane. He judged what could be shared and what couldn't be. Hard, decisive Kane. Black-and-white Kane. If the ship was sinking, he would be the first to shove women in the lifeboats, regardless of whether they preferred to die with the husbands they loved. Because he didn't love and he didn't understand love.

He didn't measure the gin into the glass, simply splashed a generous amount over the ice.

"What's wrong, Kane?" Lissa asked quietly.

He flashed her a mocking little smile as he poured tonic water over the gin. "Oh, just about everything," he drawled.

Lissa felt as though an iron fist were squeezing her heart. "So why did you come home?"

"I had to talk to you. And I couldn't do it over the phone," he said flatly.

Lissa's hand slid over her stomach as she thought of what she wanted to tell him, face to face, but this was clearly not the time.

He brought her her drink.

She took it, clutching the glass hard to stop her fingers from trembling. She looked at his stony face, tried to probe the black eyes, and failed. "What do you want to talk about, Kane? Now that you're here in person," she said as calmly as she could, hiding her turbulent emotions.

"I need to know about the Wingicamble Project, Lissa," he stated, his voice gravelled with harsh urgency. "I need to know. And I need to know it now!"

He hadn't come home for her. To be with her. He had come home because his business was at risk and she could fix it for him. A wave of nausea rolled through Lissa's stomach. He hadn't taken her in his arms and kissed her or made love to her because she was totally secondary to what meant most to him. First things came first.

Stupid to feel so upset, her mind pointed out on some detached level. Kane had told her the truth before he had asked her to marry him. He would choose his business ahead of her. That knowledge did not stop her heart from weeping tears of blood. She lifted bruised eyes to his, purple with the internal haemorrhaging of her love.

"Is this why you married me, Kane? So that you could get the information from me if you needed to know?"

She had suspected it when he had proposed, dismissing the suspicion because she hadn't wanted to believe it. Jack Conway had suspected it. To him it had made the kind of sense he used himself. Lissa had blindly persisted with the thought that Kane was different from Jack Conway. That she really meant something to her husband.

She watched Kane's reaction to her question almost as though she were an onlooker, outside this scene. His face tightened. Anger blazed from his eyes. Or was it frustration? Lissa felt she was dying inside, her senses becoming anaesthetised. She couldn't tell what Kane felt. Had she ever been able to tell? her mind mocked.

"For God's sake, Lissa!" he burst out violently. "This is for us!"

"Is it, Kane?" she retorted coldly. "I seem to remember I married you for richer or for poorer. It was totally irrelevant to me whether you were a success in your business or not."

"You're my wife!" he argued fiercely. "I married you because I wanted you as my wife. And I expect my wife to take my side when I need the help she can give me. Is that too much to ask?"

He hated asking her, she realised. It scraped his pride raw. He would not have done it unless he was cornered, fighting for survival. But, of course, he had always known it was a contingency weapon that could save him. *One more day,* she thought. *Just one more day and Jack Conway would have called him, and I would never have known that Kane had married me for this.* What bitter irony!

"I gave my word to Jack Conway that I wouldn't tell you," she stated flatly.

"Jack Conway." Kane jeered the name. "Do you imagine, for one moment, that your word would mean anything to him if he could twist it around to his advantage? This game is played by winning, Lissa," he stated harshly. "Jack Conway knows that. I know it. Everyone who's ever got anywhere knows it. And you know, as well as I know, that he plays you as a card in his game."

Kane gave a contemptuous laugh and turned away to refill his glass with whiskey. "Your word," he drawled. The black eyes flashed bitter mockery at Lissa. "I bet he enjoyed that. He loves having the power of yea or nay over men like me. And you know why, Lissa?"

It was a rhetorical question. He needed no encouragement from her to go on. "Because he envies us. He hasn't got the guts to get out from the protective wing of a giant corporation and put his own neck on the line. Oh, no! Jack Conway likes it safe."

He tossed back a hard swallow of whiskey, then faced Lissa again, his eyes glittering with derision.

"There's only one problem with that, Lissa. He has the power, but not the profits. And that sours Jack Conway inside. He doesn't want to put his neck on the line but he resents the success of those who do, because he knows the profits involved. Which are more than his pay-packet will ever amount to, despite his exalted position."

What Kane was saying was probably all true, but as far as Lissa was concerned, it had nothing to do with her. She didn't care about the power games that men played. She cared only about the marriage she didn't have.

Kane dropped his voice to a softer, persuasive tone. "Don't you think you owe me more loyalty than you owe him, Lissa? My neck is on the line right now. It's our future that's at stake. His isn't."

Not our future, Lissa mentally corrected him. His precious business. If Kane loved her, their future wouldn't be at stake at all. They would ride out whatever happened, good or bad.

"To me, it's not a question of loyalty, Kane," she answered bleakly. "I've always placed a lot of store by integrity, my integrity."

Red slashed across his cheekbones. His black eyes shone even more brilliantly above the uncharacteristic colour. "It's not a matter of integrity," he denied savagely. "I'm not about to use the information to harm ICAC in any way. I simply need to know so I can plan which way to move. If the Wingicamble Project isn't coming to me, Lissa, I've got to take desperate measures *now* to save what I can. If it's mine, I've got room to manoeuvre.''

When she didn't respond, he banged his glass on the counter and stretched out both hands in an appeal to reason. Kane could reason anything away, Lissa thought. It was reason that drove him to do whatever he did, even to marrying her. Cold, unfeeling reason.

''Lissa, the decision has been made. Has to have been made by now. It's only a matter of time before ICAC announces which tender has been accepted for the contract. It will make no difference to ICAC whether I know now. No difference whatsoever!''

Calm, clear logic, cutting through her argument about integrity, cutting right through to her heart and stabbing to death any hope of him loving her. He started to walk towards her, his hands still outstretched. She could see him deliberately relax his facial muscles, softening his expression.

''Do I sack my men or keep them, Lissa?'' he asked softly. ''There's a lot of jobs on the line. I can carry them if we've got the Wingicamble Project. I can't if it's not coming up. It'll be a hell of a mess if I sack my men and then have to try to rehire them.''

She was still holding the drink he had given her. Kane took the glass from her hand, placed it on the nearest counter. He was going to try physical persuasion, Lissa thought. Everything within her recoiled against such a hypocritical move from him. He didn't love her. He hadn't pushed his business aside for even a few moments to kiss her hello after three weeks of absence.

As he turned to her, her eyes flashed him a hard warning. "Don't, Kane!" she bit out icily.

He frowned. "Don't what?" she asked.

He knew. He stood still, the black eyes probing hers with urgent intensity. Looking for vulnerability, Lissa thought. Not tonight, husband dear, she promised him. Her bleeding heart did not have the strength to overrule her head tonight.

"Why bother coming home?" she mocked. "Why didn't you ask me over the telephone this morning? Surely that would have been more practical and economical?"

He grimaced, a mixture of vexation and frustration. "You wouldn't have liked that, Lissa."

"I haven't liked you being away from me for three weeks, either, Kane. But that didn't persuade you into coming home for a night. I presume it is only a night. You have to go back tomorrow."

"Yes. As for my not coming home before this, I did explain the situation to you, Lissa."

She nodded. "Business first. It always has been. It is now. And that's not going to change, is it, Kane? You came home for the sake of your business—"

"*Our* business, Lissa," he interrupted emphatically.

His hand lifted towards her face. She stepped back, her eyes flaring with fierce rejection. "Don't touch me, Kane. You didn't come home to make love to me. Don't you dare start now, or we're finished. I think we're finished anyway. But if you want any chance with this marriage, don't push your luck, because it's on the line, as well as your precious business."

His face tightened. His black eyes blazed with furious pride. "What the hell does that mean? I asked you for help and that's the end of our marriage?"

"You hate it, don't you? You hate asking me for help," she accused bitterly.

"Yes," he hissed.

"Marriage is about sharing, Kane. Sharing the bad as well as the good."

"Isn't that what I'm doing with you now?" he answered resentfully.

"Only out of necessity. To save your business."

His fist thumped on the counter. "*Our* business, dammit!" he shouted, then worked to get his passion under control. His voice seethed with impatience as he went on. "How many times do I have to say it? This affects our future, Lissa. Don't you care about that as much as I do?"

"Yes, I care. I care too much," she cried. Tears blurred her eyes. "I gave my word to Jack Conway, just as I gave my word to you on our wedding day, Kane. If I don't keep one promise, what are my other promises worth? What does trust mean if it isn't absolute? I thought it meant something to you. I thought it was because you could trust me that..."

She choked up.

"Lissa," he pleaded, then shook his head in anguished conflict. "I *need* to know...."

He would know tomorrow, she thought with dull resignation. That was soon enough to save his all-important business.

"Go back to Melbourne, Kane. It's not too late to catch an evening flight," she said, icy death crawling through her veins.

She couldn't bear to be with him a moment longer. Her whole body reacted with revulsion at the thought of him staying the night with her. She turned on her heel and made for the stairs, forcing her shaky legs to work to her will's dictation.

"Lissa . . ."

She ignored the harsh plea in his voice. She didn't need any more words from him. Didn't want them. She understood all too well, and the understanding made her feel more ill than she had ever been in her life.

"Lissa," he called again, more urgently.

Her stomach heaved. She was going to be sick. Somehow she managed to push her legs faster. She had to get upstairs to the bathroom before she disgraced herself. Pride insisted that Kane not witness her distress. She heard his footsteps on the stairs, following her. He called her name again. She made it to the bathroom ahead of him and frantically pushed the lock on the door. Then she staggered to the bowl and retched until her stomach had nothing more left in it.

She heard Kane pounding on the door, calling out to her, but whatever he was saying was shut out by a ringing in her ears. Her skin was clammy. She was frightened she was going to faint. She sat on the edge of the bath, slumped forward, fighting the dizziness.

There was an almighty thump, then a splintering crack as the lock gave way. The door crashed open and Kane filled its space, his face as black as thunder, his whole body heaving with turbulent feelings. Reason shot to pieces.

"If you don't want to be touched, do you think I would touch you?" he yelled at her. "There's no need for locked doors between us! There never will be a need for locked doors in our marriage! God damn it! What do you think—"

The torrent of angry words came to an abrupt halt as he took in her white face and limp body. He sucked in a quick breath and his tone dropped to a shaky note of concern. "Lissa? You look... Why didn't you tell me you weren't well?"

She looked up at him with dull, bleak eyes. "It apparently goes with the condition."

He shook his head, not understanding, disturbed by alarming uncertainties. "What are you talking about?"

Her mouth took on an ironic twist. What a way to tell him! No joy now. No happiness to look forward to. No beautiful togetherness. Simply a fact to be faced.

"I'm pregnant."

She saw the realisation dawn that this was what she had wanted to tell him tonight, but he had been too full of his own problems to give her the opening. An anguished regret twisted across his face. Perhaps hav-

ing a child—*his* child—was more important than his
damned business, Lissa thought. But not her. *She*
wasn't important to him. She was simply the means to
an end. Both ends. *His* business...and the bright new
life he wanted for *his* child.

He came and crouched beside her, the dark eyes
filled with pained appeal. "I'm sorry, Lissa," he said
in a soft, husky voice. "I've spoiled it all for you,
haven't I? Tell me how I can make up for it."

It totally undermined the little control she had left.
Hopelessly weak, she thought, as tears welled into her
eyes. She couldn't speak. Her throat ached. Her whole
body ached for the loving she had wanted from him.

Kane didn't wait for a reply. He gathered her in his
arms, holding her gently, tenderly, his lips brushing
softly over her hair as he carried her into the bedroom and laid her carefully on the pillows. He tucked
the quilt around her. He brought a cloth and wiped her
clammy forehead. He made her a cup of tea and
coaxed her to drink it. He cooked her a light fluffy
omelette and brought it to her on a tray, watching her
in anxious concern as she did her best to eat it.

Nursing her, she thought in ironic bemusement, remembering his contempt for Trevor Woodbury for
doing precisely the same thing for his sister. Then she
realised it was not her Kane was nursing. It was the
baby he cared about, the child of his seed inside her.
She was simply the woman who would give birth to it,
the mother of his child, and as such, she had to be
looked after.

Yet he was so contrite, so concerned, and Lissa was so starved of some show of caring from him, that she weakly accepted it all, not even protesting when he slid into bed beside her and cuddled her against him as though she were a baby to be comforted and soothingly caressed.

"Lissa." Her name was a murmur of torn wanting in the darkness. "You were right. I should not have asked you to betray any trust. If you were not what you are... That *is* important to me, Lissa. Please don't think I don't value the kind of person you are. There's only ever been you, only you for me to believe in...."

Her heart almost broke from the sheer force of the tidal wave of feeling that rushed through it. She couldn't speak. Her emotional relief ran too deep. She might not have his love, but at least she had earned his trust, his faith, his respect.

Kane made no move to break his careful restraint with her. It was she who lifted his hand to her breast, she who turned in his arms to bring his head down to hers, she whose mouth provoked passion from his, she who moved her body to accommodate both of them when she had aroused the desire for more and more intimacy. She wanted him, needed him, loved him, and at least she could have him physically, she told herself.

She cradled his head against her breasts as he kissed them, his tenderness all the more sweetly erotic because of their taut sensitivity. She stroked his strongly muscled shoulders as he trailed his lips lovingly over her stomach. My child as well as his, she thought fiercely. The baby they had made together. Rightly or wrongly. It was done. Too late to break the commitment she had made, no matter if Kane never loved her.

But he made love to her beautifully. There could never be a better lover than Kane, she consoled herself. Waves of intense pleasure washed through her body. It was easy to forget what she didn't have. Kane made it easy for her to forget everything but what he could make her feel, and when he finally slid inside her, what did anything else matter? Dear heaven! This was the beginning and end of life itself. Kane...

He cradled her against the slumbrous beat of his heart in the sweet aftermath of passion. At least she was his woman, his wife, and that couldn't be taken away from her, Lissa thought, hoarding the comforting satisfaction in her own heart. Why she loved Kane so much, Lissa didn't know. She wondered if Jenna knew why she loved her brother, or whether love had no reason at all.

*I had to protect Kane....*

Jenna's words slid into Lissa's mind and wouldn't let her fall asleep. With a flash of insight, she realised that love narrowed choices, creating an overriding influence that diminished personal interest to something meaningless. The whole essence of it was in giving, regardless of one's feelings.

Jenna would not have stayed with her mother and stepfather if she had had only herself to consider. Not weakness, no! Lissa had seen that inner core of strength in Jenna, the strength that was born of love to suffer anything if it meant a better chance for the one she loved.

Kane had offered that to his sister. He would have given up his education for her. Jenna had decided to sacrifice herself rather than let him do that. It had broken her. It had lost her the brother she loved because he hadn't understood her sacrifice. He was repulsed by it and would never have accepted that tragic gift of love had he known.

Perhaps only a woman who loved would understand...a woman who knew instinctively that love was about giving.

That was why Jenna had expected her to understand.

Lissa did now.

While Kane no longer wanted her to sacrifice her integrity, there was something she could give him without betraying any trust.

"Kane?"

"Mmm?"

"Jack Conway said he was going to call you tomorrow. He didn't ask me to promise not to tell you that. So you'd better catch an early plane in the morning. Be there for the call. It's...it's important to you."

A long breath wavered through her hair. "You mean... I'll know what to do about the men tomorrow?" Kane asked gruffly.

"Yes. But I'd rather you act as though you didn't know the call was coming."

He held her more tightly, more possessively. "Lissa, believe me, I won't ever do anything to hurt you, not knowingly."

There was a deep ring of sincerity in his voice. Lissa did believe him. Kane couldn't help being the way he was, but he truly didn't mean her any hurt. She was his wife. And that did count for something. It meant quite a lot to Kane, Lissa realised with a sudden surge of contentment. He simply didn't know—or understand—about some things. Like with Jenna....

It wasn't right that Jenna had to suffer the estrangement from Kane on top of everything else she had suffered. Lissa vowed to fix that somehow. She was giving Kane his child. One way or another, she would make Kane give Jenna her just due. Lissa would not let him wipe his sister out of their future. Jenna had earned her place in their family.

Justice, Lissa thought. There had to be justice. Kane might never understand love, but he had an acute appreciation of justice.

# CHAPTER TEN

JACK CONWAY MADE the all-important call the next day. Kane telephoned Lissa soon afterwards to share the good news with her and to tell her he would be home for the weekend. For Lissa, that weekend was like a second honeymoon. Kane had got what he wanted, about his business and about having a family straight away. It made all the difference in the world to their marriage. The way Kane treated her was almost exactly what every woman could want from her husband.

As it turned out, Lissa could not keep her job for long. Although Kane unexpectedly said to do whatever she felt happiest with, she simply didn't feel well enough to give her best to her work, and she handed in her resignation only a fortnight after learning of her pregnancy. On hearing the reason she wanted to leave, Jack Conway congratulated her rather ruefully and let her go without holding her to the required notice.

Most mornings Lissa was violently nauseated, and during the day there were spells of dizziness. Her mother recommended a cup of tea and a couple of biscuits before getting out of bed in the morning. That did seem to settle the worst of the nausea. The dizzy feeling was similar to the motion sickness she used to get in a car when she was a child. Lissa found that sucking candies helped. A bit.

Kane bought jars and jars of them. Lissa had such a variety and such a store of candies that she figured they would last her through several pregnancies. However, she accepted Kane's indulgent extravagance without demur. It was his way of looking after her as best he could. He also brought her the cup of tea and biscuits every morning when he was home. Which was most of the time during the early months of her pregnancy.

She couldn't help remembering that Kane had once scoffed about bringing her a cup of coffee every morning, saying it wasn't his idea of love. But her well-being had become his prime concern. Lissa didn't fool herself it was out of love for her. It was for the child she was carrying, the child whose birth would herald Kane's clean, new life.

Nevertheless, she didn't let that prey on her mind too much. After all, it was heaven being the focus of Kane's loving attention, even if it only lasted until the baby was born. She would face that when she came to it, Lissa decided. Perhaps, by then, Kane would have come to love her, and not only because she was the mother of his child.

Lissa did not forget Jenna. The problem remained in the back of her mind, waiting to be resolved when the best opportunity presented itself. She kept thinking about how Jenna and Trevor could be drawn into their family, yet the more she thought about it—the kind of problems it raised—the more she was inclined to let the matter slide. Justice did not necessarily produce happiness.

For one thing, Trevor was not Kane's type of man. Lissa couldn't see them becoming friends. Apart from which, it could be that Kane and Jenna were better off apart. Lissa had seen how painful the past was for both of them, and visiting each other would probably keep bringing it back to them. Which neither of them wanted.

Jenna was happy with Trevor. Kane was certainly happy with Lissa at the present moment. Let sleeping dogs lie, Lissa told herself. What had happened between brother and sister was a deep business that had nothing to do with her, and she doubted that she would be thanked by either party for interfering.

Lissa was four months pregnant when the accompanying sickness finally subsided and she had the pleasure of feeling really well again. As part of a checkup on the baby's progress, Lissa's doctor sent her for an ultrasound. The baby was fine, and to Kane's intense pride and joy, the scan showed that he was going to be the father of a son. He didn't stop grinning all day.

It was over dinner that night, with Kane still beaming deep pleasure, that the thought of Jenna slid into Lissa's mind again. Sharing good news with her family had always been so natural to her that the words spilled off her tongue before wiser considerations could cut off the impulse.

"Your sister would like to know, Kane. Why don't you call her and..."

The change in Kane's expression brought Lissa to a faltering halt. He frowned at her, questioning her judgment and accusing her of treading on ground that should not exist between them.

"Jenna has nothing to do with our life together, Lissa," he said in his soft, dangerous voice.

Lissa could feel the heat rising in her cheeks as the need for safeguarding her happiness with Kane fought with her sympathy for his sister. Common sense dictated that she back down. Fast. And yet...

"She telephoned here when you were in Melbourne. It was embarrassing for me. I had to explain that we were married. And..."

"Why did she call?" Kane broke in curtly.

"I don't know. Hasn't she been in touch with you since then?"

"Since when exactly?"

"It was four weeks after our wedding. I remember because she asked."

Kane gave a sharp dismissive shake of his head. "I haven't spoken to Jenna since last Christmas."

"Oh!" Lissa's cheeks burnt more painfully as she realised why Jenna had been so circumspect about meeting her. Desire had overwhelmed discretion on both their parts. Lissa felt constrained to confess what she had done. Better for Kane to know now than to find out and think she had gone behind his back. "I didn't know you were that much out of touch. Jenna asked if I would have lunch with her. And I did."

His mouth twisted into a savage grimace. "What on earth possessed you to do that?"

He wasn't being fair, she thought. Cutting himself off from the only family he had was one thing. Forcing her to be cut off, as well, was quite another. He had placed her in an intolerable position. On the grounds of any normal humanity, meeting Jenna had been the right thing to do. No matter what Kane thought, Lissa didn't regret doing it, either. She faced him squarely and listed her reasons.

"Because she asked me. I thought she might need help. And she's your sister. I felt terribly guilty that she hadn't been invited to our wedding. And embarrassed that she hadn't been told of our marriage. I saw no harm in meeting her. I wanted to."

"That must have been quite an experience for you," he mocked. "I hope your curiosity is now satisfied. Skeletons aren't pretty when they come out of dark cupboards, are they?"

Bitter Kane, hating the skeletons, hurt by their intolerable existence, wanting them kept locked in the dark cupboard where he had put them.

Jenna didn't have a chance with him.

He had made his judgment, and that was that.

Whether he was right or wrong, Lissa didn't know, but she couldn't help feeling it was unfair. Tears rushed into her eyes. She seemed to be overemotional these days. Something to do with hormonal imbalance, the doctor had told her. She didn't want an argument with Kane, so she pushed herself up from the table and began gathering their plates.

Kane shot to his feet, took the plates from her, dumped them on the table. She looked at him tremulously. He wrapped her in his arms and held her close to him.

"I'm sorry," he rasped. "I've made you feel bad, and you've just given me the best day of my life." He planted warm little kisses around her temples, then drew back enough to lift his hand and tenderly brush the tears from her cheeks. He gave her a rueful smile. "It's not that important, Lissa. I know you meant well."

"Kane..." She swallowed hard, took a deep breath and spilled out what she felt. "I know it's none of my business, but I thought Jenna was a lovely person. She was happy for you that you'd found someone you wanted to marry. She seemed to understand that you didn't want her in our life. It made her sad. I thought she would like to know about the baby. If you don't want to tell her..." She shook her head as more tears flooded into her eyes.

Again he gathered her close, gently pressing her head onto his shoulder. "Don't cry, Lissa," he said softly. "If you want me to tell Jenna, I will," he agreed, stroking her hair and back as she struggled to regain composure. "I ought to call her away. Maybe there is something she needs. I'll do it now if you like."

"Yes," she choked out. "If you don't mind. I didn't mean to interfere, Kane."

"I guess it's not something I can expect you to understand," he said with some pain. "It wasn't part of your world. God knows, I wouldn't want it to be part of anyone's world.''

''I'm sorry,'' she whispered.

''Don't worry about it. You're not to worry about anything,'' he commanded. He tilted her head, gave her a long kiss, then sat her down in his chair. ''I'll get you a cup of tea. You sit and take it easy, Lissa.''

He gathered up the plates and headed for the kitchen with brisk purpose. Lissa did not argue. She felt absurdly shaky. Not strong at all, she thought, wryly correcting Jenna's judgment of her. Having a baby was not as straightforward as it was supposed to be. If it wasn't messing her around physically, it was messing her around emotionally. She didn't seem to be on top of anything. But it did bring out the best in Kane, she thought appreciatively. Which balanced things up on the positive side.

He brought her a cup of tea, dropped a kiss on her wobbly smile, then went straight to the telephone.

Lissa had no shame whatsoever about listening to Kane's side of the conversation. Whatever he felt towards Jenna, nothing could restrain the pride in his voice when he announced that they were expecting a baby and it was going to be a boy. Although Lissa suspected he would have been just as proud if it had been a girl. A child of his own flesh and blood, that was all that mattered to Kane. Now the baby she carried had become a real person to him, identified as a boy.

There was a long silence while Jenna gave her response. Whatever was said had some noticeable effect on Kane's voice. "Thank you, Jenna," he said huskily, then cleared his throat before asking for the reason she had telephoned when he'd been away.

Several minutes went by with only a few meaningless words from Kane to break his sister's long passage of speech. His voice became curt, Lissa noticed. He obviously didn't like what he was hearing. She heard him say yes a couple of times in quick succession, then he hung up.

She looked towards him expectantly, but Kane was off in another world. Lissa knew instantly that there was trouble afoot. Kane's face was tightly drawn, his eyes black fathomless pools, focused inward. Violence emanated from every line of his body.

"I have to go out, Lissa," he announced.

"What is it, Kane? What's wrong?"

"Nothing wrong. Something I have to check," he clipped out. "Don't wait up for me. I don't know how late I'll be."

"Would you like me to come with you?" she offered, knowing it had to be something to do with Jenna.

"No." Hard and decisive. He came over to her, squeezed her shoulder reassuringly, dropped a kiss on her forehead. "Take care of yourself," he admonished, then left without another word.

It might not be anything to concern her, but Lissa worried about it all the same. Some problem had arisen that had driven the baby right out of Kane's mind. It had to be a big problem. Yet Kane had denied that something was wrong, and Kane scorned lies.

Lissa wished she had not mentioned Jenna tonight. The day, and the night, had very definitely been spoiled.

Despite Kane's instruction that she was not to wait up for him, Lissa tried to, until she couldn't keep her eyes open any longer. Her pregnancy seemed to rule when she had to sleep, even demanding she take naps in the afternoon. It also woke her up in the middle of the night with a pressing need to go to the bathroom.

Kane was not beside her when she woke. A glance at the bedside clock showed two-seventeen. Lissa visited the bathroom, then felt too ill at ease about Kane's absence to go back to bed. This was not late. It was very, very late. She put on her dressing gown and headed downstairs to heat up some milk, thinking she would sit up for a while. Surely Kane could not be out for much longer.

She quickly discovered he was not out at all. He was in the living room, nursing a glass of whiskey. A half-empty bottle sat on the low table in front of him. He hadn't heard her come downstairs. He was totally enclosed in a dark, brooding world of his own.

However much alcohol he had consumed, it had certainly not relaxed him. A tense, explosive air shimmered from him, as though he desperately wanted to fight but the phantoms that taunted him were out of his reach. The grim look on his face was carved from deep and bitter frustration.

"Kane?" Lissa called softly, a little frightened by his intensity and wanting to draw him to her and the world they shared.

He looked up abruptly, frowning at her. "Why aren't you in bed, Lissa?"

"I woke up. You weren't there. I was worried."

"There's nothing to worry about. I don't feel like sleeping yet. That's all." He roused himself and stood up. "Can I get you anything?"

She shook her head, and instinctively moved towards him as she spoke. "What's wrong, Kane? Please tell me."

"Nothing wrong," he denied, then gave a harsh, derisive laugh. "Jenna gave me some good news." The black eyes glittered with pain that he couldn't quite hide. "You want to hear the good news, Lissa?"

She nodded, coming to sit on the sofa with him, hoping she could help in some way, if only by touching him, letting him know she was there for him. But Kane did not sit down again. He moved restlessly over to the fireplace on the far wall and propped his elbow on the mantelpiece. His face twisted in savage mockery as he spoke.

"Those apologies for people who posed as our parents were not our parents. Jenna and I were adopted. She's not my sister, either. No blood relationship between any of us."

Lissa swallowed the shock of those bald statements as Kane gave another harsh little laugh.

"I always thought it was one of Jenna's fantasies. Something she wanted to believe. But it's true. Trevor had all the papers there to prove it. He got access to records through his job. He believed Jenna's fantasies. And he was right to believe them."

He gave a twisted smile to Lissa. "They had the proof when Jenna telephoned here and found out about you. She said she realised then that I wanted to cut completely clear of the past, so she thought it was better not to bring it up at all. But tonight, when I told her about the baby, she thought it was important for me to know that our child bore no blood relationship to those animals."

He lifted his glass in a mock toast. "Joy to the world! It is now considerably cleaner! And that is the good news!"

But there was no joy in him. He did not feel cleansed at all, Lissa realised. The hatred he had borne his so-called parents burned even deeper, blackening everything. She watched him swallow another gulp of whiskey and said nothing. Kane was hurting badly.

"Trevor and Jenna had it all worked out. And finally... Yes, finally it makes sense," he said bitterly. "The eminent Professor Marriott was in a position to choose us as interesting subjects for an experiment. Different sets of genes, opposing characteristics. Me naturally aggressive, Jenna naturally passive. Heredity versus environment. Objects to be tested to see what would happen. That's all we were, Lissa...guinea pigs."

He made a sound of disgust and threw his head back as though mentally crying out against the fate that had placed them in such cruel hands. "And to think I pleaded with him! Pleaded with that monster to save Jenna!"

His gaze swept to Lissa, his eyes black holes of endless pain. "He wasn't interested in saving her. He wanted it to go on. And they told her... They told her if she ran away I'd suffer for it. That's why she stayed and took what was done to her. And I blamed her for it, Lissa. I was furious with her for being so weak."

He shook his head in heart-wrenching anguish. "Weak...my God!"

"You weren't to know, Kane," Lissa offered as some appeasement. "It seems to me that your feelings for each other were manipulated to create the greatest stress. And that's why you were sent away to school to deepen the sense of helplessness that hurt you more than anything else."

"But I let the bastards win, Lissa!" he cried in self-contempt. "Jenna and I had stuck together until then. We had a bond between us that we wouldn't let them break. But I let them break it. I thought she'd let me down, but it was I who betrayed her. I turned my back on my little sister and—"

"It wasn't your fault, Kane!" Lissa broke in with passionate conviction. "And you didn't turn your back on Jenna. You've helped her all these years...."

He shook his head. "All I've done is try to get her out of whatever messes she landed herself in. I didn't give her what she needed from me, Lissa. I couldn't..." There was despair in his voice as he revealed the worst truth. "I couldn't feel it any more."

They had drained him of all feeling except hatred, Lissa thought. It was hatred that had sustained him through those years. And the burning need for jus-

tice. It had been a crippled love that had sustained
Jenna until she knew that love wasn't there for her any
more. Then she would have destroyed herself, except
that Trevor had saved her with his love.

Lissa understood the burden of guilt that lay so
heavily on Kane's soul, and she tried to lighten it for
him. "Jenna survived. You survived," she pointed out
softly. "And it's not too late to change what was done,
Kane. You don't have to stay cut off from your sister.
We can bond Jenna in with our family. If you think
she'd like that."

"Lissa..." He flashed her a look of hopeless rejection, then paused, searching her eyes as though wondering if there was such a possibility, if it was feasible.
"I know how you feel about family, Lissa, but Jenna
isn't really my sister. You don't have to feel
obliged...."

"Kane, she *is* your sister. You were adopted as
brother and sister, and that bond is still there, despite
all that's happened. I have no problem with Jenna.
When I met her, I truly thought she was a lovely person."

He frowned, as though not quite able to bring himself to believe her. Then his lips curled into an ironic
little smile. "Jenna thought you were a lovely person,
too. She liked you very much."

Lissa tried a teasing smile. "That's because you
married me. Jenna would think anyone her brother
married was a lovely person. Otherwise you wouldn't
have married me. And don't criticise that logic, because I quite like it."

He relaxed a little, his eyes glinting with a sparkle of warmth for her. "Jenna's judgment isn't all bad," he agreed. He heaved a wry sigh, then added, "In fact, it's starting to look better than mine. I always thought Trevor was a wimp. But he's not."

"I thought he was very nice. And very good to your sister."

Kane nodded. "He's always been that. I used to think..." He grimaced. "I was wrong. He's okay."

Which was probably as high an accolade as Kane would give to another man.

Kane's face tightened into grimness. "You were right, Lissa. Jenna was happy about us having a baby. She can't have children herself. She got an infection that left her sterile."

That bleak piece of news hit Lissa like a blow. Her hand instinctively moved to protect the child she carried. How devastating it must be to any woman to know that she could never have a child! To someone like Jenna, who had so much love to give....

Kane took another swig of whiskey then banged the glass on the mantel. "I hope there is a God. I hope there is a Judgment Day. And I hope they burn in hell for eternity for what they did!"

"Don't let them take any more from you, Kane," Lissa said quietly. "They're not worth remembering. Not worth another second of your life."

She rose from the leather sofa and walked over to where he stood. She looked up at him, her violet eyes as soft as velvet, pleading against the hardness in his. She reached up and stroked his cheek imploringly.

"When you asked me to marry you, you said that our life would be whatever we made of it. So let's make it good. And make it as good as we can for Jenna, too. We could share our child with her, Kane. At least we could try, couldn't we?"

Appreciation and admiration slowly warmed his expression. He lifted his hand, covered hers, then moved her palm to his lips. He pressed a kiss on it, then smiled at her.

"I did get something right in marrying you, Lissa. You're all I need and want, and to have you at my side . . . It means everything to me."

Lissa knew she didn't mean everything to Kane. Nor did she provide him with all he needed and wanted. But it was probably the closest Kane would ever get to a declaration of love. Her heart fluttered happily. Her head shut down on thinking any more.

"Let's go to bed now," she said.

"Yes," he agreed, sliding his arm around her and hugging her close to him.

Making love was a good way to end a day.

Or to begin a new one.

# CHAPTER ELEVEN

LISSA HAD ONCE THOUGHT Kane would never change. Marrying him had been the most dangerous gamble she had taken in her life. Yet, over the later months of her pregnancy, she began to realise and appreciate that following her heart and instincts, instead of her head, had not been wrong. Kane Marriott was a good man with a good heart. Essentially he always had been. His withdrawal to the sidelines of humanity was simply for self-protection—where no-one could get at him any more.

Perhaps it was a need to have someone with him on those lonely sidelines that had motivated his proposal of marriage. Her insistence on not being cut off from her family had seeded the first change in him. Meeting her parents had shown him how life could be for them if he tried hard enough. The reality of Lissa's pregnancy had seeded another change, rearranging his priorities. His child's life was more important than anything else. Finally the revelations of his adoption and Jenna's sacrifice for him wrought other changes in Kane.

He became much less judgmental, far more ready to look at other points of view, to appreciate the good in people, instead of standing aloof from them. The barriers he had set around himself were gradually lowered. He began to reach out more, give more of himself not only to Lissa but to those close to them.

Her family warmed to him, particular her nearest brother, Tony, who frequently dropped in to visit when he was home from his overseas flights. Jenna and Trevor also became welcomed visitors, sharing the occasional Sunday lunch with them.

Lissa's family was happy about the baby, but to them a pregnancy was a normal, natural occurrence in a marriage. As the birth drew nearer, Lissa grew more and more conscious that to Kane and Jenna, it was of momentous significance. To Lissa's mind, it represented too much to them, as though all the goodness of life was embodied in the baby to be born.

In one way it was heart-warming, in another it was slightly disquieting. Lissa began to feel less like a person and more like a vehicle for Kane's son, particularly in the last couple of months when Kane started to refrain from lovemaking because it might somehow upset things. Lissa could hardly complain about any lack of caring for her. Kane treated her as though she were fragile crystal. Yet she could not help feeling she had definitely slipped to second place.

Perhaps it was feeling cumbersome and unlovely that put her in a depressed state of mind. She wanted Kane to tell her that he loved *her,* that it was *she* who made all the difference to his life, not the child she was about to give him. There were times she felt jealous of the baby, and on many occasions it was extremely difficult not to snap at Kane for being oversolicitous about what she was doing or how she was doing it.

She longed for the pregnancy to be over, yet was frightened she might feel even more jealous of their child when Kane could actually hold his son in his arms, separate and apart from her. As much as he might want and need her beside him, Lissa felt she would never achieve the kind of intimate bonding with Kane that he would share naturally with his son.

Kane would be there for his child, right from the beginning, whereas he had never been like that for Lissa. There was so much of her life that was entirely different to Kane's. No sharing ground at all. There had been a bridging across that chasm of misunderstanding, but with his son there would never be a chasm. Kane would make sure of that.

Lissa told herself she should be grateful he was intent on being a good father. She was grateful. She just wished that being her husband meant a bit more to him.

The week the baby was due, there was trouble at the Wingicamble Project and Kane was in Melbourne. Lissa felt weak, gross and depressed. Kane had stressed that if the baby showed any signs of coming, she was to call him immediately. That was the cause of the depression. She knew beforehand what the result would be. Wingicamble was more important than holding her hand. If he did come, it would be because of the baby, not because she needed him by her side.

She guessed her life would always be much the same. Kane would always be off somewhere, building projects that very few other people could tackle. He would be nice to her, good to her, and he would shower all his love on his son and whatever other children they had.

He telephoned her each morning and night to check if anything had happened yet. Lissa had no complaint about Kane not thinking of her, although she knew it was more the baby on his mind. Jenna called. Lissa's mother called. Everyone kept checking up on her. She heartily wished the baby would make a move so all the fuss would be over and done with.

Kane had been away for four days when the first positive notice of imminent birth occurred. Her water broke. Lissa rang her doctor, who advised her to go to the hospital right away, even though Lissa had not felt any contractions. They would soon start, he promised her.

She dialled the number Kane had given her to call during work hours, wanting to share her excitement with him but mentally preparing herself for disappointment if he was tied up somewhere.

I'm supposed to be strong, she told herself. Strong enough to do without the emotional support of her husband. Women had been having babies all throughout history without husbands by their sides. To actually be together was a relatively recent social development. It wasn't necessary. Besides, Kane had seen enough pain, anyhow. Better to share the joy afterwards. It was the reasonable thing to do.

Apart from which, Lissa was only too aware how critical it was to Kane's engineering company that the Wingicamble Project went ahead as smoothly as possible. In a material sense, their future security was at stake. For herself, that didn't matter so much, but she did want the best opportunities in life for her children, just as Kane did.

A woman answered the call, and when Lissa asked to speak to Kane, she was told he was in an important meeting and wouldn't be available for some considerable time. If she would like to leave a message...

Lissa took a deep breath to quell a silly rush of tears. "Tell him that his wife called and—"

"His wife!" The woman instantly became flustered. "Oh, Mrs. Marriott, is it the baby? I mean... Oh, dear! I'm terribly sorry. It's just that we all know Mr. Marriott has been on pins and needles waiting for a call from you and... Oh, dear! I shouldn't be gabbling on. I'll put you through to him immediately. Hold on a moment, Mrs. Marriott."

Lissa barely swallowed her surprise that Kane's staff was informed of his private and personal situation when his voice came over the line, tense and urgent. "Lissa? What's happening? Are you all right?"

"Yes. I'm fine, Kane."

She was barely through her explanation of the circumstances when he broke in with, "I'll join you at the hospital as soon as I can get there. Leaving now, Lissa."

She could hardly believe her ears. "What about your meeting? It'll probably be hours and hours before—"

"Lissa, I'm coming now," he said decisively. "Everything else can wait."

Lissa was amazed that being with her for the birth of their son was absolutely top priority. Apparently everyone close to him had been made aware of that all along. Except her. Perhaps he had taken it for granted that she knew. She shook her head in bemusement as she put the telephone down. Even if it *was* because he didn't want to miss out on his son's birth, Kane was going to be with her all the way. She breathed a sigh of blissful happiness.

Lissa almost felt like a fraud when Kane turned up at the hospital a little over three hours later. The contractions—if they could be called that—were so weak that she had been advised to walk up and down the corridor to get things moving. That was where Kane found her.

He arrived like a whirlwind of tense anxiety, enveloping her in a careful hug, the dark eyes glittering with excitement and apprehension. ''What are you doing out here?'' he asked, ready to criticise anybody and anything and make things right for her.

''I think our son must be lazy,'' she teased, loving Kane's concern for her. ''He's not pressing to be born, and I'm trying to urge him on. The sister said walking would help.''

Kane relaxed. He smiled. ''Well, at least he had the good judgment to wait for his father to get here. Are you in any discomfort, Lissa?'' he added caringly.

''None at all,'' she assured him.

Nor was there any marked discomfort over the next two hours. Lissa began to feel that nothing was ever going to happen, but Kane was wonderful to her, bringing her cups of tea and keeping her company. Her doctor finally decided to induce labour. She was put on a bed and given an intravenous drip of pitocin. This was supposed to bring on the contractions, and it did.

Over the next four hours, Lissa had good reason to be grateful for all the antenatal classes she had attended. The breathing exercises helped her to ride through the pain of the contractions. Kane, however, grew more and more distressed as time went on, and Lissa had to keep reassuring him that everything was all right.

The doctor came by to check her again and looked non-committal after his examination, which disturbed Kane even further. The decision to give her an epidural block was welcome, in so far as it relieved Lissa of all pain, as well as helping the dilation process necessary for natural childbirth to progress.

There was some limited success with this process but it didn't work well enough. More hours went by, hours of frustration, exhaustion and growing panic. Prenatal classes hadn't prepared Lissa for anything going wrong, and it was plain that something was very definitely not right.

More and more doctors came by, encouraging Lissa to push with the contractions. She was wired to monitors so that the baby's heartbeat could be continually checked. No matter how hard she tried to do everything she was advised to do, her body simply did not, or could not, cooperate with what was meant to happen. Kane did his best to keep her calm and soothe her fears, but his own enforced composure cracked hard and fast when the baby's heartbeat became irregular.

He demanded action and got it. Suddenly there were several doctors continually in the room reviewing the situation. They quickly reached the conclusion that the baby could not be born naturally—a case of cephalo-pelvic disproportion. A caesarian operation was the only option, and since the baby was now in distress—critical distress—it had to be delivered as fast as possible.

The epidural block had been administered too low down for the operation, and she had to be put under a general anaesthetic. Lissa was ready to agree to anything if it meant saving the baby. The strain on Kane's white face told its story of how much that meant to him.

Kane walked beside her as she was wheeled towards the operating theatre, holding her hand tightly, grimly. His dark eyes seemed to beg hers for an assurance she couldn't give him. She felt helpless, a failure as a woman, a failure as his wife. It was now sixteen hours since she had been admitted into the hospital, and their baby son's life was at risk.

Lissa had a sinking feeling that what she meant to Kane was also at risk. If the baby was lost... If she couldn't have any more children... If this was their only chance for the clean new life he had envisaged... ''Tell me you love me, Kane,'' she pleaded in a hoarse whisper, desperately wanting some assurance that she was important to him, aside from the children they might not have.

''Lissa...'' He seemed to choke up, staring at her in pained disbelief that she should ask such a thing at such a moment.

Then it was too late for him to answer her. He was asked to stand aside and Lissa was wheeled into the operating theatre. It wasn't supposed to go wrong, she thought despairingly. The anaesthetist started chatting to her about the latest movies he had seen. Such a stupid, frivolous thing to talk about—movies that meant nothing—when the real life she wanted was in the balance—both lives, her baby's and her own with Kane. Or maybe it would never be real, only what might have been.

Kane's son....

His and Jenna's clean new life....

It wasn't fair. No justice, no justice at all....

Wasn't there some return for loving?

Then consciousness rapidly slipped away, and Lissa felt nothing more.

BLACKNESS. BLACKNESS everywhere. She couldn't see anything, couldn't feel anything.

I'm alive, Lissa thought.

The baby.... What about the baby? She seemed to struggle for a long, long time. She felt no pain. Slowly, sluggishly, her eyes opened to light...and Kane's face hovering over hers.

"The baby?" she asked, fear sweeping through her, choking her.

"Thank God you're all right!" The taut concern on his face relaxed as his head bent lower, his mouth moving in soft kisses over her forehead, his hands tenderly splayed across her shoulders.

Lissa fought a mounting sense of apprehension. What had happened to her baby? She tried to ask, but nothing came out. No words. She couldn't breathe. Her hands came up to check her throat. Nothing.

Nothing. She saw Kane's head jerk back, his face twisting with frantic anxiety as he saw her choking, fighting for breath. Any breath. She heard alarms going off. Kane shouting, "Get a doctor!"

She couldn't breathe . . . couldn't! Nothing!

"Laryngal spasm," someone said.

A nurse held a mask over her face. Lissa fought it, not understanding, desperately needing freedom to breathe and knowing a mask couldn't possibly help. This time I'm going to die, she thought.

Did Kane have his son?

She wanted to know, wanted to find out if she had failed him. But there was no way she could find out. Tears welled into her eyes. Not knowing.

Vaguely, somewhere in the distance, she heard Kane screaming, "Save my wife!"

A jab in her arm.

Some awful thing being forced into her mouth.

A strange sensation of floating, which was quickly obliterated by the blackness of nothingness.

I'M STILL NOT DEAD, Lissa thought in surprise. I must be like a cat. Nine lives. Two gone. Seven to go.

She opened her eyes to light again. Not the recovery room. Intensive care. Kane watching her with burning intensity, his eyes black, glittering coals, unwavering, focused only on her. She felt his hands curled gently, warmly, around hers. She tried to smile at him, didn't succeed. Her mouth was dry.

Kane looked haggard, unkempt, his hair all awry, his tie hanging loose and screwed around, top buttons of his shirt undone as though he, too, had been choking. The whites of his eyes were bloodshot. A thick shadow across his jaw. He was leaning forward, hovering over her like a clucky hen.

"Lissa, Lissa," he was murmuring huskily. "You're going to be all right. Oh, Lissa...."

A sheen of moisture making his eyes more glittery. Why didn't he tell her about the baby? He appeared so discomposed. It had to be bad news. He was keeping it from her. She had failed him.

"I'm sorry," she whispered, her heart aching with a bleak rush of despair.

"Oh, God!" he said. It seemed to send him into a spasm of anguish. His hands tightened around hers, squeezing in agitation. "I need you so much, Lissa," he rasped. "I love you. I'll never stop telling you I love you. I love you, I love you...."

Kane distraught, fighting for control. Lissa remembered asking him to tell her he loved her just before going into the operating theatre. Somehow it did not reassure her now. The important question was still not resolved.

"My baby...?"

"You're not to be worried. Not to be stressed. Just take things calmly. Everything's all right," he choked out.

"Tell me...about the baby." Knowing the worst was better than not knowing anything. Didn't he understand that?

Kane finally recognised she had to be put at ease on this vital point, and concentrated his mind briefly on it. "I'm sure the little scoundrel is fine," he said dismissively. "You're not to worry about him, Lissa. Don't worry about anything."

Hope and relief mixed with uncertainty as she considered Kane's answer. "What do you mean you're sure he's fine? Don't you know?"

"Well, they put him straight into a humidicrib to make sure he was fine. So I guess he is. I couldn't leave your side."

"Kane!"

Her cry alarmed him. "You must stay quiet, Lissa."

She took a couple of deep breaths, then spoke as calmly as she could, but her violet eyes flashed with darkly purple determination. "Kane Marriott, you go and find out *immediately* what's happened to my baby."

"Lissa . . ." Anxious protest.

"Immediately!"

"I'll get a nurse to sit with you."

"Immediately!"

"You're not to be left alone."

"I'm getting very upset, Kane."

"I'll go immediately."

He hurried off, but a nurse did turn up to sit next to Lissa. She wore an indulgent smile as if she was doing something totally unnecessary.

"I'm all right," Lissa croaked.

"Yes, dear," the nurse replied, giving her a piece of ice to suck. "But when your husband has that look of black murder in his eyes, it doesn't seem wise to say no to him." Her smile turned a little lopsided. "I think if he'd lost you, the world would have ended for quite a few other people as well. He, uh, doesn't take to being told what to do, does he?"

The nurse was right. When Kane made up his mind, that was that. There was still a lot of black and white in Kane, although he had softened considerably. Lissa suspected the hospital staff hadn't seen much softening.

"Has Kane been disrupting things around here? Breaking some hospital rules?" she asked tentatively.

"All of them!" the nurse replied with a resigned sigh. "He doesn't trust anyone to look after you properly. I don't know how you got him to leave your side. No one else could."

"He loves me," Lissa said, finally realising it was true. Kane did love her. In his way. He was not the greatest communicator in the world—not verbally—but his actions spoke volumes about loving her. And needing her. She was more important to him than their son.

"You're not wrong about that," the nurse said dryly. "In fact, no-one's been left in any doubt about it."

Kane reappeared, coming at a fast stride. It seemed to Lissa he had barely been gone for five minutes. His gaze instantly fastened on her in urgent reappraisal, checking that nothing had happened in his absence. The nurse quickly displaced herself so that Kane could sit by Lissa's side again.

"Well?" Lissa asked anxiously.

"Oh, he's okay."

Another dismissive reply. Lissa glowered at him in disapproval. After all she had been through, she wanted to know more about her baby than that. Besides which, Kane couldn't have possibly made a proper examination of their son in barely five minutes.

"Is that all you have to say?" she demanded.

"He's fine. Really. He's fine," he said urgently to soothe her.

Lissa began to suspect that Kane hadn't gone to check on the baby at all, that he had only pretended to, or asked a nurse to. "Describe him to me," she commanded.

"Well, there's a lot of hair. Very black."

Also very predictable, since they both had black hair. "Yes?" she persisted inquiringly.

"And he's kind of red."

"You're not very good at description, Kane," she chided.

He tried harder. "His head's a funny shape...."

"Oh, my God!"

"Not to worry, Lissa. They tell me it will come back to normal in a few days. It was because of the pressure... being stuck for so long in the birth position before the delivery," he hastily explained.

That made sense. Babies' heads were soft. Lissa relaxed again. "What else?" she asked.

Kane shrugged. "It's hard to see details. He's in a humidicrib with about twenty wires attached."

Lissa's nerves leapt in alarm. "Is he in danger?"

"No, Lissa. No danger," came the swift assurance. "They're just monitoring him. All babies from caesarian births are put straight into humidicribs because the fast delivery causes a drop in body temperature and they need time to adjust," he recited.

"How long does he have to stay there?"

Kane frowned. "A few hours."

"Hasn't he been born for more than a few hours?"

"Well, they don't need his humidicrib for any other baby. I think it's a good idea that they make damned sure his heartbeat is okay. Which it seems to be. But there's no harm in keeping watch."

Lissa suddenly had a mental image of all the nurses and doctors in attendance on Kane Marriott's son having been given a vivid impression of black murder in his eyes if they didn't keep watch. Kane Marriott was a man who made his presence felt when it meant something to him. However, he couldn't be in two places at once. While he had done what he could to safeguard their child, he had chosen to keep watch over her.

"I see," she murmured, a huge flood of love for him billowing through her heart. "Is there anything else?"

"He's got one of everything he should have one of, he's got two of everything he should have two of and he's got five of everything else," he said decisively.

Kane had not yet mastered people skills, but Lissa had no doubt about his counting ability. Her smile held a touch of wry indulgence. "You are hopeless, Kane Marriott."

"Yes," he agreed seriously. "Without you, I am. And you're not to scare the life out of me again, Lissa. You had me looking straight into a black void that I just can't face."

"I'm sorry," she said softly. She knew all about that black void. Without Kane. . . .

"And it's because I love you," he declared with absolute conviction.

"Yes," she murmured, believing him beyond a shadow of a doubt, believing him because his love for her was in his eyes, in his voice, in the arms that slid around her and held her safe, in the mouth that kissed hers with a tenderness that cherished her beyond anything else.

"I love you, too, Kane," she whispered, and kissed him back, her heart and mind in ecstatic harmony.

KANE'S DESCRIPTION of their son was completely wrong. He was not a little scoundrel at all. He was an adorable baby with chubby cheeks and dark blue eyes and his head was definitely not funny. It was covered with beautiful fluffy black curls.

Once Kane was convinced that all danger to Lissa was past, he slowly thawed from being offhand about their child and began to adopt the role of proud father. After a few days, the little scoundrel graduated to being a son worth having, so long as he wasn't interfering with Lissa's well-being. Which brought home to Lissa how much her dance with death had meant to Kane. Life was suddenly so much sweeter, especially now that she knew Kane loved her.

Her family called at the hospital to visit them and offer their congratulations and good wishes, but the visit that meant most to Lissa was from Jenna. Lissa felt overwhelmed by the love that poured from Jenna as she cradled the baby she would never have. The way she held it to her heart so tenderly, the look on her face. . . . It was as though a baby was the source of all joy and wonder and beauty.

"He's perfect, Lissa," Jenna said with a blissful sigh.

"Will you be his godmother, Jenna?" Lissa asked impulsively.

"Oh, yes!" Her lovely soft face lit up with a luminous smile. "I think I'm getting better, Lissa. I'm not so frightened of people any more. I promise you I'll be a good godmother."

"The best," Kane agreed, putting his arm around his sister's shoulders and giving her an affectionate hug.

Lissa silently sent up a prayer of thanks that everything had turned out right. Looking at the three of them, Kane and Jenna and the baby, Lissa felt the pain of the past had finally been put to rest for them. As well as it could be.

The future looked brighter still a few days later when she questioned Kane about the Wingicamble Project. "Don't you have to go back to Melbourne?" she asked.

"No. I've got Jack Conway taking care of things," he answered, blithely playing with his son's fingers.

Lissa shook her head in disbelief. "You've got the managing director of ICAC doing your work for you?"

Kane nodded. "He's good. Knows the management game inside out. Doesn't compromise when he shouldn't." He lifted his gaze to hers, the dark eyes flashing warm appreciation. "You showed me I should give people more of a chance, Lissa. I offered Jack Conway a partnership. He decided to take it last week. The day before sonny boy here interrupted everything."

"He took the partnership?" Lissa couldn't imagine Jack Conway out in the field. To her, he belonged behind his big executive desk.

"Sure, he did. He was getting jaded at ICAC. This is a new challenge for him. And a real share in profits. Besides, it's a no-risk venture now." Kane grinned in happy anticipation. "Gives me more time to spend with you and this little scoundrel."

And the family they would have, Lissa thought in glorious contentment. The doctor had assured her that there was no reason she couldn't have more children. They would have to be caesarian births, but the problems she had encountered this time would not be repeated. She was one of the unfortunate few who had a severe reaction to the drug that was used. Now that her condition had been diagnosed and documented, everything would be quite straightforward in the future.

Of course, she wouldn't talk about that to Kane for quite a while yet. He was still getting over the fright of almost losing her. But time healed most things. Particularly with a lot of loving.

Kane leaned over and kissed her. "I forgot to tell you. I was in a meeting with Jack when you called. He said to give you his best wishes."

Lissa shook her head in bemusement. Strange how one thing led to another!

Kane lifted her hand and rubbed it against his cheek. His eyes were black velvet, caressing her with love. "We're going to have a good life together, Lissa."

"Yes," she agreed, brimful of happy confidence.

He pressed a warm kiss into her palm, then slid it over his cheek again. "I was once determined never to need anybody," he confessed ruefully. "When I met you, Lissa, I wanted you, but I still told myself I didn't need you. Until that weekend you said we were finished. Then suddenly I couldn't bear the thought of you going out of my life." He pulled a self-mocking grimace. "I didn't handle that very well, did I?"

"In your usual aggressive way," Lissa teased indulgently. "And I kept telling myself I was a fool to put up with it." She took his hand and pressed it to her cheek. "But I'm glad I did, Kane. All we needed was a period of adjustment."

He shook his head. "Not you, Lissa. Me. You've changed me for the better. And Jenna," he said huskily. "I'll never be able to match what you've done, what you've given me. But I'll try my best to give you all I can. Always."

He had been trying, Lissa knew. For a long time. Everything had changed. She came first. Their family came second. Business came last. Most important of all, Kane had learnt to love her, as she loved him. They had survived. Together.

"Always love me, Kane," she whispered.

To Lissa, that was the answer to everything.

HARLEQUIN PRESENTS®

# BARBARY WHARF

### Home to the *Sentinel*
### Home to passion, heartache and love

The BARBARY WHARF six-book saga continues with
Book Two, BATTLE FOR POSSESSION. Daniel Bruneille
is the head of the *Sentinel*'s Foreign Affairs desk and Roz
Amery is a foreign correspondent. He's bossy and
dictatorial. She's fiercely ambitious and independent.
When they clash it's a battle—a battle for possession!

And don't forget media tycoon Nick Caspian and his
adversary Gina Tyrrell. Will Gina survive the treachery of
Nick's betrayal and the passion of his kiss...?

**BATTLE FOR POSSESSION (Harlequin Presents #1509)**
available in November.

October: BESIEGED (#1498)
If you missed any of the BARBARY WHARF titles, order them by sending your name, address, zip or postal code, along with a check or money order for $2.89 for each book ordered (please do not send cash), plus 75¢ for postage and handling ($1.00 in Canada), for each book ordered, payable to Harlequin Reader Service, to:

| In the U.S. | In Canada |
|---|---|
| 3010 Walden Avenue | P.O. Box 609 |
| P.O. Box 1325 | Fort Erie, Ontario |
| Buffalo, NY 14269-1325 | L2A 5X3 |

Please specify book title(s) with your order.
Canadian residents please add applicable federal and provincial taxes.

BARB-N

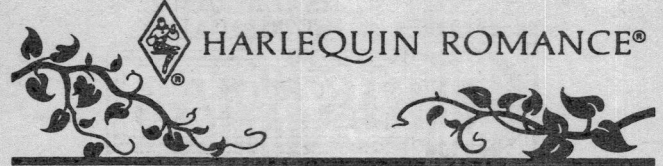

# HARLEQUIN ROMANCE®

**Harlequin Romance
invites you to a
celebrity wedding—or is it?**

Find out in Bethany Campbell's
ONLY MAKE-BELIEVE (#3230),
the November title in

# THE BRIDAL COLLECTION

**THE BRIDE** was pretending.
**THE GROOM** was, too.
**BUT THE WEDDING** was real—the second time!

Available this month (October)
in The Bridal Collection
TO LOVE AND PROTECT
by Kate Denton
Harlequin Romance #3223

Wherever Harlequin Books are sold.

WED-7

## · HARLEQUIN · HISTORICAL

# CHRISTMAS

### · STORIES · 1992 ·

Capture the magic and romance of Christmas in the 1800s with HARLEQUIN HISTORICAL CHRISTMAS STORIES 1992—a collection of three stories by celebrated historical authors. The perfect Christmas gift!

Don't miss these heartwarming stories, available in November wherever Harlequin books are sold:

**MISS MONTRACHET REQUESTS** by Maura Seger
**CHRISTMAS BOUNTY** by Erin Yorke
**A PROMISE KEPT** by Bronwyn Williams

Plus, this Christmas you can also receive a FREE keepsake Christmas ornament. Watch for details in all November and December Harlequin books.

**DISCOVER THE ROMANCE AND MAGIC OF THE HOLIDAY SEASON WITH HARLEQUIN HISTORICAL CHRISTMAS STORIES!**

HX92